First edition: November 2020

Illustrations copyright © 2020 by Priscilla Bampoh
Book cover and design by David Bushay
Edited by Elanor Best

ISBN: 978-1-8382576-0-6

www.leahosakwebooks.com

NONNY'S
BIRTHDAY BASH:
CONFETTI & CATASTROPHE

1

What do you do when your mum tells you that you can throw a huge party for your thirteenth birthday, complete with a DJ *and* the cake of your dreams?

You jump up and down on your bed for at *least* ten minutes, scream "WOOHOO!" until your voice is hoarse, then flop onto your back, out of breath and dizzy with joy.

Well, that's what *I* did.

I'm Nonny, and my thirteenth birthday is just around the corner. It's in June: the *best* month of the year. June means the start of summer and the countdown to the end of boring old school (I can almost *taste* the freedom!). It means fruity ice lollies, barbecues in the back garden, my birthday and *now*... MY PARTY!

EEEEK – I can barely contain my excitement! Not just because I get to throw my *first ever* birthday party, but because I'm finally going to be a teenager! Hopefully this means that my parents will let me live a little and stop treating me like such a baby. Even my besties, Georgia and Nyah, are allowed to stay out later than me and go to the town centre on their own. It's not fair – their parents are *way* more laid-back than mine.

When we go to Georgia's house, her mum buys us popcorn and sour sweets and lets us stay up for as long as we want! She even lets us watch films that are for fifteen-year-olds, but I'm not allowed to tell my parents that.

And Nyah's parents give her EVERYTHING she wants. Her dad drives us anywhere we want to go, music blasting so loud it makes my teeth chatter. And her mum lets us borrow her fancy clothes and jewellery and pretend we're on a catwalk. Sometimes when I lay in bed at night, I imagine me and Nyah switching bodies so that I become the only child of fun, rich parents with a glamorous lifestyle.

But me? I'm barely allowed to do ANYTHING. My dad is bossy and grumpy, and my mum is just… strict. They make me come home straight after school while everyone else gets to hang back and go to the park, or the cinema or anywhere else where *cool* people with *cool* parents go. I can't even watch TV until I've done my homework! I've tried, but the vision of my angry dad's flared nostrils and raging eyes behind his glasses has put me off for *life*.

Sometimes if my dad's not home yet and my mum is too busy fussing over my little brother to notice me, I can creep downstairs and sneak in a couple episodes of my favourite show. But then I hear my dad's car tyres crunching on the gravel, and it's a race against time to switch the TV off with lightning speed and sprint upstairs to "do my homework".

It *sucks*. All my dad cares about is homework, chores and getting top marks in school, and I've got the captain of the Fun Police for a mum. She says no to *everything*.

When she's *really* fed up with me, her eyebrows wrinkle up and she shakes her head from side to side so her chunky gold earrings jangle. That happens at *least* every other day. So, you'll understand why having a party is such a HUGE deal. She *finally* gave in!

Every year it's been the same. At exactly four weeks before my birthday, I plan my attack. I wait until she's in a better mood than usual, then I sidle up to her, my palms sweating and my heart racing. My mouth opens, and out tumble the same ten words.

"Mum... please can I have a birthday party this year?"

"No."

"But *whyyyy?*"

"Because no."

"Pleeeeease! I'll do all my chores and-"

"No."

This year was just the same. Four weeks before my birthday, like clockwork, I crept up beside her in the kitchen on a Saturday afternoon. She'd just been shopping, so her hair was pulled back into her usual, elegant bun and she was wearing her favourite ruby-red lipstick (I've pinched it more times than I can count, puckering my lips in the mirror and pretending to be a grown-up. Luckily, I remembered to put it back in her makeup bag this time!). She was making lunch for my three-year-old brother, Isaac, and humming along to the music on the radio.

Perfect timing.

When she hums like this, it means she's happy, which is usually because Isaac hasn't thrown a tantrum. And on this occasion, it meant she also hadn't noticed that I'd broken a plate and hidden it at the bottom of the bin.

I took a deep breath. *Three-two-one:* "Mum… please can I have a birthday party this year?"

First, there was a deathly silence. You could almost hear my stomach churning. Then, she turned to me and smiled.

"Okay. Since you're about to be *thirteen.*"

Did she just say what I think she said? My eyes

squinted with suspicion. My forehead creased with confusion.

"R-really?" I stuttered. (I was careful to not ask too many questions, just in case she changed her mind.)

"Yes."

My mouth flew open in shock. She actually said YES!

"Thank you, thank you, thank you!!! Thank you SO much!" I cried, throwing my arms around her waist and squeezing tightly. She smirked and shimmied out of my grip.

"Don't make me change my mind."

"I won't, I promise!" I sang.

I was about to dance out of the kitchen and up the stairs when it hit me. I had a *party* to plan! There was so much to do, and I had some burning questions that just couldn't wait a minute longer.

I turned to my mum and asked timidly,

"Sooo... does that mean I can have a DJ? And the cake I've always wanted?" My eyes twinkled with hope, thinking back to the first time I saw that giant chocolate fudge cake in the bakery window. It had THREE tiers and it was HUGE; I had to strain my neck just to look up at it! Since that day, I've longed for a birthday cake *just* like it. I love chocolate fudge cake, but I want to choose my *own* flavours – red velvet, lemon, and salted caramel. *Mmmmm!*

She sighed. "Yes, Nonny."

I gasped and clapped wildly. "YESSS!"

As soon as I'd skipped up the stairs and bolted into my room, I shut the door, jigged on the spot like a crazy lady and... the rest is history.

Now it's Monday and I cannot WAIT to tell Georgia and Nyah. I just have to tell them in person so we can all hug, scream and get planning immediately.

We meet at our spot by the potted plants every morning. Today, I half-skip, half-run over to them, beaming from ear to ear. I'm so excited to spill the beans.

Georgia and Nyah are my best friends of all time. We've been inseparable since we were in primary school. Although we're quite different now, we'll always have that special bond. We've even got a secret, three-way handshake. And we stick together no matter what.

"Guess what, guys?!" I grin, interrupting their conversation about the film Georgia saw at the weekend.

They both turn to stare at me, scanning my smiling face for clues. They've probably never seen me this happy on a Monday morning.

"*What?*" they cry in unison.

"My mum said I can have..." I pause for dramatic effect. "A PARTY!" I shriek.

Georgia's mouth opens so wide I can see every one of her teeth. Nyah squeals so loud that Mrs Brown shushes her aggressively as she walks past. We all glance at each other and collapse into uncontrollable giggles. When we eventually come up for air, I feel such excitement I can barely stand still.

"*Sooo,* who's coming?" Nyah smirks, tapping the tips of her fingers together like a cunning mastermind with an evil plan.

"Obviously not *The Witches,*" Georgia cuts

in, pretending to stick two fingers down her throat.

"Of course not!" I gasp in horror.

Ugh – Amber Wartsworth and Becky Ritchcraft. Otherwise known as The Witches. Well, that's what Georgia, Nyah and I call them. They're *horrible*. They're the most horrible girls in school.

Of course, there are others. Like Lisa. She's pretty scary, with a cold, unfriendly glare that sends shivers down my spine. And there's Sana. We used to be close in primary school, but then she blossomed in all the right places and left our friendship in the past, along with our limbless Barbie dolls and all the juicy secrets we shared.

Still, NO ONE is worse than The Witches. Just the thought of them makes my insides jump, flip and somersault. They're definitely NOT invited to my party.

Amber Wartsworth is the ringleader. I'm convinced she was brewed in a cauldron before she was born. She makes it her mission to make *everyone's* life a misery, including mine, Georgia's and Nyah's.

Ever since Year Seven, she hasn't stopped on her quest to embarrass or intimidate her victims. She cackles about people's appearance, plots evil schemes and spreads vicious rumours.

Like the time she told that awful lie that Nyah had wet herself during P.E. That whole day, anyone who walked past us would pinch their noses in disgust, whoop with laughter and scuttle off in a flash. Not all of them were trying to be nasty. I think a lot of them were just pleased that they weren't the butt of the joke this time. Nyah tried to confront her.

"Why did you tell everyone that about me, Amber?"

"Tell everyone what?"

"You know what! That I wet myself!"

"But… you did."

"No, I didn't, you horrible liar!"

"Oh, *waaaah!* Don't start crying. Just because you're embarrassed that you wet yourself, doesn't mean you should take it out on me!"

"You're… you're… you're so NASTY!"

"Maybe you should buy some nappies. I'm sure you don't want that little *accident* to happen again, do you?"

"Well, maybe *you* should buy some manners!"

"Pffft, no thanks. Now, get out of my way, loser."

"No!"

"I said… get out of my way."

"No wonder no one likes you. You're a horrible person."

"Boring. You said that already. Now move."

"Well, it's true-"

"MOVE!"

And that was that.

Amber loves to cause trouble and make people sad – but what makes it worse is that she's… pretty. Like *really* pretty.

Her angelic features and sky-blue eyes make all the boys fall at her feet. Her halo of long, golden tresses makes parents and teachers think she's so sweet and innocent. *Ugh* – her nails are *always* filed to perfection, and her porcelain skin is flawless. Not a spot in sight. Sigh. You either despise her, or you want to be her. Or both.

Her evil sidekick, Becky Ritchcraft, is always right by her side. Becky wants to be *just* like Amber. She straightens her mane of rebellious curls nearly every day, and wears the shiniest lip gloss she can find, just so she can try and stand out next to her. It's so obvious that she wears a push-up bra, too.

She's always slightly out of sync when her and Amber strut into the classroom together, or a few seconds behind when they try to spew their cruel comments at the same time. She looks to Amber for approval before she says anything on her own, as though she can't *bear* to slip up in front of her master. Although she's nowhere near as scary as Amber, she's still a nightmare. Like when she stuck her foot out as I walked past her in the canteen, then screamed with glee as I slipped with sheer panic in my eyes and fell with a loud THUD in front of *everyone*.

The whole place erupted into laughter while my face burned with shame. Georgia and Nyah helped me up as fast as they could, then I ran to the toilet and sobbed in the cubicle for the rest of lunchtime.

Now do you see what I mean?

"... And you'll need a chocolate fountain, of course. And donuts! Oh my gosh, and you should DEFFO get one of those photo booths that all the famous people have at their parties! Shouldn't she, Nyah?" Georgia's plump cheeks flush with excitement and the dark, loose curls in her ponytail bob up and down as she gabbles about my party.

Nyah nods passionately, but her eyes and thumbs stay glued to her phone screen. Georgia and I glance at each other, roll our eyes and sigh loudly.

"Trying to talk to you is *so* tiring," Georgia drawls.

"Yeah, Nyah, get off your phone. We're trying to talk about my party!"

"Yeah… yeah… I'm coming. Just wait a second."

"That's all you ever say! 'Wait a second, I'm coming, hang on.' *Hello?* Can't you hear us talking to you?" Georgia snaps, waving her hand in front of Nyah's face.

"Oh my gosh, would you WAIT?! I'm just replying to *one* message. Hang on!"

"How about replying to us for once? Your best friends? Or have you forgotten that we exist, yet again? You're literally *obsessed* with your phone. I bet you don't even *know* the person you're talking to right now," Georgia jabbers, shaking her head.

"Yeah, I'm coming. Wait a second," Nyah mumbles.

Georgia's right. Nyah's ALWAYS scrolling through her phone, howling with laughter at the latest funny post, or squealing with delight when one of her many internet crushes likes her photos. Sometimes she doesn't even listen because she's too busy chatting to her online "friends" and taking countless selfies for her page. (Though, to be honest, if I looked like her, I would take hundreds of selfies too.)

Her dimples soften her face when she smiles, and she's *always* got the freshest braids, inspired by all the glam celebrities she worships online. Nyah's so lucky; one month her silver braids will flow all the way down her back, complementing her dark skin like an ebony goddess. The next, they'll sit pretty in jet-black at her shoulders, crowning her perfect face.

"NYAH!" Georgia shouts, grabbing Nyah's phone from her manicured grasp.

Nyah gasps and snatches her phone back, giving Georgia one of her famous dirty looks.

"WHAT? I said yes!" she barks.

I guess Nyah and I are quite similar when it comes to being distracted. But while Nyah is *obsessed* with her phone, I just gaze into space and fall into my own secret world. My mum's always telling me to focus, and my school reports say the same thing. It's not that I don't *want* to listen. It's just that I can always imagine myself somewhere better, somewhere more exciting.

One minute I'm listening to Mr Barker drawl on about next week's test, and the next, the words on the whiteboard are merging into squiggles and shapes, and *POOF*, I'm on the beach in Jamaica – my dream holiday destination.

I'm definitely the quietest out of my friends, which can be so frustrating when I meet new people. I would love to make new friends, too. Not that I don't love hanging out with my two BFFs, but how cool would it be to get invited to *other people's* sleepovers and trips into town at the weekend? It's a shame I get shy so easily.

Especially when I'm around Daniel.

He's my crush. When I see him, my legs turn to mush and my heart skips a beat. Luckily, you can't see me blushing through my caramel complexion, otherwise I'd have tomatoes for cheeks whenever he's around.

Most of the other boys at school behave like animals. They shout and playfight in lessons, and sometimes they even lift girls' skirts up then run away! But Daniel is different. He's kind. He's clever. *And* he's quiet – just like me.

His curls are always neatly trimmed and his braces glint when he speaks.

I don't even think he knows my name and we've never actually spoken before, so I have *no* idea how I'm going to invite him to my party. I'll probably take one look into his dark brown eyes and become a stuttering mess.

Ahhh, I just *hope* he can come!

"So, what are you gonna wear?" Nyah asks, tucking her phone into her blazer pocket and grabbing my arm excitedly.

"I have no idea, but it *has* to be amazing."

"It will be! We can help you, can't we, Georgia?"

"Yeah, for sure! You should wear a playsuit. Actually, no, you should wear a mini skirt and one of those really nice one-shoulder tops that everyone wears!"

"You know my parents would *never* let me wear a mini skirt, Georgia!"

"Okay, fine. What about a crop top and jeans?" Nyah proposes.

"There's NO WAY I'll be allowed to wear a crop top either! Whatever I wear can't be short *or* tight," I sigh.

"Well, *that's* boring," Nyah says.

"Maybe you can wear something you've

already got. I bet you've got *loads* of clothes you could wear," Georgia muses.

I picture all the clothes sitting in my wardrobe: denim skirts, t-shirts decorated with hearts and flowers, fluffy jumpers. Nope – I'm going to *have* to convince my mum to buy me something new, unless I want to look like a ten-year-old on my first day as a teenager.

"I'll figure something out," I shrug.

Nyah's eyes light up and she grins widely. "Let's get planning."

COUNTDOWN TO MY PARTY: 4 WEEKS

2

I'm so tired this morning. The dark bags under my eyes could carry ALL my mum's shopping. When I'm this tired, it's usually because my parents and Isaac are snoring like animals and I've stolen my mum's tablet to watch late-night American TV until my eyes are sore. Or it's because I'm up past midnight chatting and gossiping with my two besties. But *this* time, it's because I decided to start writing my birthday party list. WOOHOO!

On The Big Day, I want EVERYTHING to be pink and purple: my favourite colours. The cupcakes will be coated in lilac frosting and topped with dainty little flowers made out of pink icing. The balloons will be pink and purple, and the confetti will be bright pink. I'll have marshmallows, candy floss, pink wafers, EVERYTHING! I've written it *all* down.

I love writing lists. They make me feel like a high-flying businesswoman who works in a tall, plush office in the city. And since I'm going to be a teenager soon, I have to be *extra* organised so that people can take me seriously. Especially my mum.

I can't do anything that might make her or my dad change their minds about my birthday party, so I'm being the most perfect daughter and helpful big sister in the world. Like on Wednesday, I texted my mum after school, asking if I could go to the cinema with Georgia and Nyah. As usual, I received a swift reply.

Mum: No.

My fingers were *itching* to beg and plead – but what did I do? I pressed my lips tightly together and typed:

Me: Okay mum

Now, *that* was hard.

Or on Sunday afternoon when my dad ordered me to babysit Isaac so that he and my mum could go food shopping. Even though I *really* wanted to go to the park with Georgia and Nyah, I smiled and said, "Yes, dad." like A Good Daughter. Obviously, I was raging inside, but I've *got* to keep up this image of me being good – at least until the day after my party, you know?

So, last night, I nestled deep underneath my duvet with a pen and an old notebook. Using my phone light as a torch so my parents wouldn't see any light under my door, I started scribbling away, focusing harder than I do at school. I was as quiet as a mouse because I *desperately* needed my parents to think I was asleep.

Nonny's birthday party list!!

- A BEAUTIFUL pink princess dress!!

- CaKE with three layers!!! I want red velvet, salted caramel and lemon cake YUMMMM! (and some candles of course)

- GIANT pink and purple balloons

- PHOTO BOOTH (OMG!!!)

- DJ!! (Me, Georgia and Nyah will make the playlist)

- A huge balloon archway to walk underneath (pink and purple balloons)

- Dancefloor maybe with a disco ball???

- Pink confetti

- Long purple paper decoration thingys

- A MASSIVE chocolate fountain

- Jam donuts

- Double chocolate brownies

- Marshmallows

- Cupcakes with purple icing and pink flowers!!

- Pink candyfloss

- Pink wafers

- Cheese and onion, ~~barbq~~ BBQ and roast chicken crisps

- BBQ chicken wings

- PIZZAAAAA!

- Lots and lots of sandwiches
- Fizzy drinks
- Pink lemonade!
- Jelly sweets and sour sweets
- A little bit of fruit (maybe some strawberries)

I was *almost* finished, but the light patter of footsteps from my parents' room made my breath catch in my throat. I cut off the phone light and shoved the notepad and pen under my pillow in record time. I tried not to crease my sacred list, but you can only be so careful when you're frantically scrambling back onto your pillow to pretend that you're fast asleep without making a sound.

I lay as still as a statue on my back with my eyes squeezed shut, trying to breathe as steadily as I could.

After what felt like hours, the footsteps FINALLY stopped. *Phew.*

I let out a long, relieved breath and let my shoulders relax. But it wasn't time to sleep just yet. I stared up at the ceiling and began to imagine The Big Day.

I'm wearing an off-the-shoulder, pastel pink dress with flouncy sleeves that ripple in the breeze. It has a tie at the waist that I pull tightly so that it fits perfectly. The skirt is just the right length – not too short to shock my parents and not too long to make me look like a ten-year-old – and if I twirl, I look just like a ballerina. Actually, a princess!

I glide underneath a gigantic archway made entirely of purple balloons and pink flowers, until I'm welcomed by a chorus of amazed ooohs *and awestruck* aaahs. *Georgia and Nyah sprinkle me with confetti while cameras flash, capturing my glamorous entrance.*

All eyes are on me. My braids float just above my waist and they're bejewelled with gold beads and pink hairclips. It's the hairstyle I've ALWAYS wanted – inspired by Nyah. I flick them over my shoulder, feeling like a diva. A thirteen-year-old birthday diva.

"Nonny, you look AMAZING!"

"Oh my gosh, Nonny, I LOVE your hair!"

"Wow, I can't believe how good you look, Nonny!"

Daniel is at the front of the crowd. His eyes transform into love hearts as he gazes at me. We catch eyes and share a moment that feels like it lasts forever.

I look around me. The dance floor is lit up and the tiles sparkle and shine. The rest of the room is covered in confetti. There are huge balloons EVERYWHERE. The music is pumping; the bass dances through my skin. Everyone is laughing, chatting, dancing, eating, taking pictures and showing the world how FUN Nonny's thirteenth birthday bash is. The people who couldn't come wish they were here. The Witches are seething, so jealous they aren't invited that they BEG to be my friend at school on Monday.

And the cake. Oh, the cake.

I check the time – 12:43am.

Sigh. Time for bed. Who am I kidding, anyway? Where on earth am I going to find a giant balloon archway? The tiled dance floor in my dreams is just the grey carpet in my living room that my mum will *definitely* make me vacuum on my birthday. And I couldn't think of anything worse than *The Witches* wanting to be my *friend*.

I slip off to sleep and before I know it, I'm awoken by the harsh beeps of my alarm. *Ughhh!* Now you can see why I'm so tired.

During History later that day, I stifle countless yawns and drift back into my dream world. It's time to pick up where I left off last night.

I rip a blank sheet of paper out of my History book and start to doodle. (I know what you're thinking – I should probably listen more in class. But at least I'm not falling asleep. *That* would be worse.)

I spend the rest of the lesson sketching three potential birthday outfits to the hum of Mr Ansah's monotonous voice. The bell rings but I'm still shading in the skirt from Outfit Three, so I stay put.

Out of nowhere, a hand yanks the paper right from under my nose. My head snaps up in shock.

Amber.

She sneers cruelly as her eyes skim the page. I know I'm no Van Gogh, but her sniggers still hurt. I'm hot with embarrassment.

"What is *this?*" she cries, passing the piece of paper to her evil companion.

Becky snorts loudly and glances quickly at Amber who nods, allowing her to speak. "This looks like it was drawn by a two-year-old!"

Why do they have to be so MEAN?

"Shut up," I mumble, trying to grab the

paper back from Becky's grip.

"*Shut up*," they mimic in unison. They glance at each other smugly, proud of themselves for actually being in sync for once.

"Give it back!" I protest.

"No way. You didn't ask nicely," Amber leers.

"Yeah, where are your manners? Didn't mummy teach you any?"

"Give my picture back, *please*," I spit.

"Nope, sorry. I'm going to keep it. Wait, why do you look like you're about to *cry*?" Amber guffaws. "Becky, look, she's about to CRY!"

"You're *such* a baby. No wonder this picture is so bad!"

"Yeah, I could draw this better with my *left hand*."

"I bet her baby brother could draw this better than her!"

"Don't talk about my little brother," I glower.

"We'll talk about whoever we *want!*"

"Let's go, Amber, before she *tells the teacher on us*," Becky drones.

My glare pierces through them like a laser beam. If looks could kill, they'd both be a lifeless heap on the floor. And I'd step over them without a care in the world, not looking back ONCE. Or if I had a superpower, I'd turn them into real witches – warts and all – so that they'd never ever be pretty again, and everyone would laugh and point at them like acts in a circus.

The Witches prance off, but not before Becky tosses the piece of paper onto the floor by my feet. I watch it fall, like a sad, dying leaf tumbling from a tree in Autumn.

As soon as they've gone, I pick it up, salty tears threatening to spill from my eyes. I crumple my artwork into a ball, feeling stupid and childish. From now on, I'll keep my ideas safe in my head or in my bedroom, where only *I* can get to them.

Ugh – I can't STAND The Witches.

COUNTDOWN TO MY PARTY:
2 WEEKS

EEEEK – not long left. My parents have been *so* busy sorting everything out in time for The Big Day. Well, I say my parents, but I really mean my mum. All my dad does is grunt and complain about "the money". I think that's because the photo booth was quite expensive. Yep… they're letting me have the photo booth! *Can you believe it?* This is seriously going to be a party to remember.

Have you ever been so excited that it's annoying everybody around you? My whole family is sick of me. I sing extra loudly in the shower and hum nonstop around the house; even *Isaac* has told me to shut up.

My dad bellows, "Get on with your homework!" when he hears me prancing around my room like a maniac. And my mum yells at me to "Be careful!" and "CALM DOWN!" when I pick Isaac up and spin him round and round in the kitchen.

But I don't care. I *never* get to be this excited about anything, especially when my parents have kept me prisoner in my own home for most of my life. The only other time I felt this fantastic was when we were jetting off to Paris. It's when Isaac was barely the size of a pip, all warm and cosy in my mum's belly. I barely slept a wink the night before, my heart beating like a drum in a marching band. That's how I feel constantly these days, and it's GREAT!

I invite my BFFs round on Sunday afternoon to get started on the playlist for my party. Now that my mum has booked the DJ, there's no time to waste. I'm going to make sure – with the help of my BFFs – that the soundtrack to the night is everything I've ever wished for. We settle on the carpet with notebooks and pens, excited to get to work.

But within minutes, there's a problem.

"I *hate* that song. Do we *have* to add it to the

list?" Georgia groans.

"It's Nonny's birthday, not yours. You added the first three songs, Georgia. Let someone else choose."

"If it's Nonny's birthday, then why're *you* so involved?"

"Why are *you* so involved?"

"Because I'm actually helping. Unlike you!"

"Stop being so selfish, Georgia. It's not all about you, you know."

"If I wasn't here, you would put the most boring songs for babies on the list. So, shut up."

"*You* shut up."

"No, *you* shut up."

"How about you just go away?"

"FINE, I WILL!"

Georgia springs to her feet, slams the notebook down on the carpet and swings the door open to leave. She stomps downstairs, furious.

I never know what to do when they argue. Whose side do I take? Do I even take sides? Most of the time, I just sit in silence, my eyeballs darting between the two of them like I'm at a tennis match.

Nyah mutters a bunch of angry swear words under her breath and starts tapping away on her phone.

I sigh. "Come on, Nyah. Let's finish this."

She doesn't budge or look up once.

"You need to speak up more, Nonny. You always leave me to look like a bad person."

The knot in my stomach twists even tighter. I really don't want to fight with my best friends, especially as we're so close to my birthday party. And I *hate* arguing.

"I know, Nyah. I'm sorry," I mumble.

She sighs and shrugs. "Whatever."

I pass her Georgia's pen as a peace offering and we get back to work in awkward silence.

When the doorknob turns, we both look up eagerly. Even though Nyah clashes with her *a lot*, I know that she loves her just as much as I do.

Georgia pads back in the room, looking sheepish. Then she takes a deep breath and turns to Nyah.

"Sorry," she barely whispers, scrubbing away at an imaginary stain on the carpet with her foot.

"Same," Nyah mumbles back. She locks her phone and sticks her hand out with her fingers stretched far apart: the cue for us to perform our special three-way handshake.

I pat the space where Georgia sat before she stormed out, welcoming her back. She grins as she sits beside us again and grabs our hands in hers. "Hopefully I won't mess it up this time!"

But she does, and we double over in hysterics as we try over and over again to get it right.

When we eventually do, and our stomachs hurt from laughing so much, we all feel ten times better.

Phew. Everything's going to be fine.

A few minor squabbles, lots of laughs and a couple of hours later, we've put together the BEST playlist you could imagine. When Georgia and Nyah leave, I read it over and over again, feeling more elated each time. WOOHOO!

Tonight is *another* late night. This time, I'm beavering away at the computer, designing my invitations! I add stars, hearts, swirls and choose a stylish font.

I excitedly click *Print* and spin around in the desk chair, patiently awaiting my work of art. But a strange noise from the printer brings my dizziness to a quick halt.

Beep, beep. Beep, beep.

I jump up, startled, and cautiously approach the beeping machine. A message flashes across the screen.

Ink is running out.
Please change the cartridge.

Oops! My dad is NOT going to be happy when he finds out I've used up all the ink in his state-of-the-art printer. Hopefully that will be *after* my party.

I gulp, press OK and watch the last few sheets of paper land in the tray. When it's all done, I pick up the wad of my invitations and grin wildly. *Aaah*, so warm and fresh and new. I can't WAIT to hand them out tomorrow.

I send a picture of the finished product to Georgia and Nyah, and within seconds my phone buzzes.

Georgia: OMG ♥ it!!

Nyah: Looks sooo good Nonny!

I smile and cradle my invitations close to my chest. I'm proud of my hard work, even if I *am* going to be a walking zombie tomorrow.

YOU'RE INVITED TO
★ NONNY'S BIRTHDAY BASH!! ★

Where? 12 York Close, Park Cross

When? Saturday 8 June

Time? 6pm-9pm

RSVP Find me at school!

DJ · Chocolate fountain
Photo booth · Lots of food!!!

 **PARTY TIME!**

I wake up on Monday morning with flutters in my chest. Today's the day. I sit up in bed and take a deep breath. It's all becoming VERY real. Soon, I'll be a fully fledged teenager, throwing the party I've always wanted. That's the fantastic part. The *not*-so-fantastic part involves giving Daniel his invitation. AAAHH!

It means I'll have to talk to him and – even scarier – *look* at him. I'm super nervous. I slip his invitation into a separate plastic wallet, protected from all the others. It might sound crazy, but I don't want it getting damaged like my birthday list (I forgot to remove it from underneath my pillow before I fell asleep, so the next day I was *not* happy). Plus, I want it to be special when I hand it to him later.

Georgia and Nyah promised me they'll help hand out invitations before lessons start, so when I reach them at our spot, I hand them a pile each. "Here are the invitations, guys!"

"Eeeek! This is so exciting!" Nyah gushes, taking her share with pride and pushing her phone into her pocket. When she puts her phone away without me or Georgia nagging her to, I *know* she means business.

Georgia clutches her wad tightly and shakes it in the air. "Woohoo, let's do this!"

"Thanks for helping. This would have taken ages if I had to do it by myself," I say.

"That's okay, Nonny. What are friends for?"

"Exactly. We'll always help each other."

I LOVE my friends. I didn't think I could feel more excited than I did last night, but I *definitely* do now.

I'm keeping a secret from them, though. They have no idea that I've tucked Daniel's invitation in between two textbooks in my bag. I know – it's weird. And embarrassing. But the textbooks will keep Daniel's invitation nice and flat so that it's in pristine condition when he accepts it. If it's all creased up, it will ruin our special moment. I want everything, *including* his invitation, to be perfect when we have our first conversation. Georgia and Nyah both know I want Daniel to come to my party *and* that I have a crush on him, but I feel embarrassed talking about how much I really like him. Anyway, Nyah barely listens at the best of times and Georgia will probably think I'm as nutty as a fruitcake because *she* says that all the boys at school are annoying. But that's because she doesn't know Daniel.

The bell rings and we go our separate ways, armed with our invitations like we're off to war.

The mission begins in French.

James and Mike accept their invitations with glee. "Thanks, Nonny!" they grin.

Sarah gives me a hug and says, "Thanks! I can't wait!"

And Frankie cheers, "Woohoo! Oh my gosh,

I'm so *excited!*"

I can't believe it – people actually want to come to my party. This is GREAT.

I head to my locker before my next lesson, invitations in hand and at the ready. *Gulp* – my next lesson is Maths. Daniel's in that class. I stick my head far into my locker, take a deep, deep breath, and secretly clasp one of my special stones to calm me down.

It probably sounds strange, but I *love* collecting stones. There's something about them that comforts me. They're not like flowers that wilt after only a few days, or chocolate that gets gobbled up in under thirty seconds (especially by me). They last *forever*. I'm always in my own little world when I pick them up, wandering underneath trees or trekking along the pavement with my head in the clouds. I only collect *cool* stones though, not those boring, gravelly ones on the side of the road that sneak their way into your shoe. Nope – only the most precious, unique ones I can find. I have them in all shapes, sizes, colours and textures; most of them are locked away in an old shoebox under my bed, but some of them are buried deep beneath a pair of raggedy PE shorts in my locker for emergencies like this.

Phew. I can just about breathe again. When my head finally emerges, I see two figures out of the corner of my eye, sashaying down the corridor like it's their catwalk. They come into focus as they get closer. I notice the lip gloss before anything else. Ugh – The Witches.

What do they want?

I hurriedly cover the stone with my shorts and straighten my back as they approach me. Before I can stop her, Amber snatches an invitation from my grasp. I reach for it, but she's quick. She stands on her tiptoes, her arm outstretched. The only way I'd be able to get it back is by jumping. That's exactly what she wants – probably so that she can trip me up when I land, then stand over me and howl with laughter. My hands flop helplessly by my sides.

Amber scans the invitation with her eyes while Becky stands behind her and squints to witness the "mess" I've created this time.

Amber starts to snigger. Becky follows suit, tittering away like a parrot on her shoulder.

"Awwww, *how sweet*. Mummy's finally letting her little loser baby have a party," Amber whines in a pretend baby voice.

Her words are like a knife to my gut. One time in Year Seven, she overheard me moaning to Georgia and Nyah that I'm *never* allowed to do anything fun, and she's been using it against me ever since. I HATE that she knows how strict my parents are.

Becky grabs the invitation from her master and reads it for herself. "A chocolate fountain?

Pfft, that's for *five*-year olds."

"Are you sure you're actually turning thirteen and not *five?*"

The Witches cackle.

I shoot them the dirtiest look I can muster and fold my arms across my chest. *"You're* not invited."

I want to sound defiant and tough, but instead, I end up squeaking like a tiny mouse cowering beneath two hungry cats. The Witches turn to each other. Their eyes widen with amusement and they both splutter with laughter.

"No one wants to come to your *dumb* party, anyway!" Amber shrieks, catching her breath. She nudges Becky with a sharp elbow, prompting her to say something extra mean.

"Exactly; it's gonna be so boring," Becky chimes in. "Only *losers* are invited!"

"Whatever. Just leave me alone. And give me

back my invitation."

"This is the most rubbish invitation I've ever seen. Who would want to come to *this* party?"

"No one! That's why no one will show up!"

I grit my teeth. "Yes, they will. You're just jealous."

The Witches crack up yet again.

"Jealous of *what? A chocolate fountain?* My mum could get that for me *tomorrow*," Amber brags.

"Exactly. Why would we be jealous? You're probably gonna be playing musical chairs and eating jelly and ice cream like a bunch of *babies*," Becky crows.

"Yeah, and wearing nappies! Especially Nyah, just in case she wets herself *again!*"

"Leave me and my friends alone!" I need them to know that I'm not a baby and that my party will be way better than what they have in mind. "And I'm having a huge *cake*, actually.

Not jelly and ice cream. So there."

"Ooooh, a *cake!*" Amber mocks. "Like *we* care. I bet it's from the pound shop, anyway."

"It's not, *actually*. I'm getting it *customised* and it's going to have three tiers," I boast, jutting out my chin. That'll show them.

I notice Becky's eyes quickly flit towards Amber. She's jealous, I can tell!

"So what, loser? We don't even *like* cake," Amber lies, folding her arms.

"Yeah," Becky echoes. "Anyway, that cake sounds *so* boring. Just like you and your weird friends."

I try not to let their words get to me. They're just jealous they're not invited – that's all.

Anyway, the only person I care about coming to my party is *Daniel*. Well, *him*, and my best friends and my DJ, too.

Just when I thought the worst was over, Becky tears my invitation in two and viciously stamps on it: I watch on, powerless. Amber shoves me as she struts past, her elbow knocking my ribs. I choke back tears. Becky looks back at me and smirks. I *hate* them.

I'm SO glad they'll be nowhere near my party to bring me down on my special day.

And at least they didn't get their grubby claws on Daniel's invitation. I tip my head back slightly to stop the tears from dropping. I can't let what just happened defeat me. I hold in the waterworks and head to Maths.

It's nearly time.

3

I can't concentrate.

I keep glancing over at Daniel from my
seat at the back of the classroom, feeling sick
with nerves. The numbers and symbols on the
whiteboard swim in front of my eyes. My hand
shakes when I pick up my pencil.

Aaahh, can this lesson be over already?

When Miss Hill finally lets us go, I let out a
long, shaky breath. I wait for everyone to get
up first, watching Chioma and Sally excitedly

re-read the invitations I handed them earlier. I reach into my bag and gently pull the invitation from the plastic as I shuffle towards Daniel, gripping the piece of paper so hard I'm scared it will tear into a million pieces. *Oh, how I wish I hadn't left that stone in my locker. I need it now more than ever!*

Daniel's packing his pencil case and calculator into his backpack. As I stumble towards him, my throat dries up and my hands get clammy. I weave through the maze of cluttered desks and narrowly miss tripping over a wayward chair.

Keep it together, Nonny!

The musty odour of ancient textbooks streams out of the cupboard, tickling my nostrils. I start to panic. What if I can't get the words out? What if I forget what I want to say?

The rest of the class bustle out of the door, chattering and pushing, excited to finally get to break. I desperately want to join them and rip this invitation into shreds; I could forget this ever happened. Daniel zips his backpack up, ready to join his friends who are waiting for him outside. It's now or never, Nonny. It's now or–

"H-hi, Daniel," I mumble, instantly regretting my decision.

My temperature immediately soars. Why am I inviting someone to my party who doesn't even know my name? WHAT AM I DOING?

He turns to me and gives me a warm, slightly confused smile. The butterflies in my stomach are having their very *own* party.

"Hey."

Ugh – just a "Hey". Not a, "Hey, Nonny".

I *knew* it – he doesn't know my name. My legs tremble. This is *so* embarrassing. Before my brain can even process what's happening, my arms reach out and wave the invitation under his nose like a flag.

He looks down at it, back up to my face, then back down again. He's confused. *Why wouldn't he be?*

"Erm, I'm, erm having a party soon," I

stammer, hearing my heart thump in my ears. *Say. Something. Else.* "Would you like to come?"

Nooo – I shouldn't have said *that*. He'll just say no!

But… he doesn't.

He nods and takes the invitation. Hopefully it's not damp from my sweaty palms. Then he smiles – *at me!*

"Yeah, I'll come. Thanks."

My heart jumps with joy. My body almost does the same, but I have to act cool, just like him. He is *so* cool. I could scream with happiness. Daniel said he'll come to my party! Daniel *looked into my eyes* and *smiled at me* when he said HE'LL COME TO MY PARTY! I could faint.

He turns and joins his friends, leaving me in the classroom on my own, grinning from ear to ear. I'd better get to break before Georgia and Nyah wonder where I am.

I plod off to meet my besties in a heavenly daze. Everything seems to be going my way. Everyone (apart from The Witches) seems to be excited about my party, and *Daniel* just said he can come! It all feels too good to be true.
But it can't be, can it?

COUNTDOWN TO MY PARTY: 1 WEEK

Saturday creeps up on me. A week to go. *Finally.* I've been feeling so antsy and restless, impatiently waiting for this weekend to arrive. Today, we buy my birthday outfit. Tomorrow, I GET MY HAIR DONE!!! I call Georgia before I get in the car.

"Hey, Nonny!"

"Hey! Guess what I'm doing today."

"Ermmm… going to the cinema? No, wait, erm…. going to the park? Oh, I don't know, Nonny. What are you doing?"

"Buying my dress!"

"Oh my gosh! WOOHOO! I can't wait to see it! I haven't even got my outfit yet. I still don't know what to wear. I was thinking maybe shorts and this really cute top I saw online. Or maybe a dress? Yeah, maybe a dress. Hmmm, what kind of dress are *you* buying?"

Sometimes, I forget how much she loves to talk. On the other hand, she's *great* at giving me the silent treatment when we fall out (which is rare, because like I said, I *hate* arguing). Like the time she ignored my texts *all* weekend because we'd had a silly fight one Friday after school. But on a normal day, she's a serious chatterbox. Just like now.

"I'm not sure yet. It *has* to be pink, though!"

"Oh yeah, definitely. Should me and Nyah wear pink too, then? Oh my gosh, we actually should. We'd all be matching. That'd be sooo cute!"

"That's the best idea ever. Let's do it!"

"Yaaay, I can't wait. I'm gonna call Nyah and tell her. Have fun shopping!"

"Thanks, Georgia. See you later."

"See ya!"

My mum drives us to the gigantic shopping centre in town, bright and early. Her long, white sundress billows in the breeze as we whiz down the road in the morning sun. I watch the trees blur into each other until I feel giddy. The dress that will help me see in my thirteenth year is just fifteen minutes away. The wait is nearly over!

Even though we've arrived early, the whole place is buzzing with the chaos of weekend shopping. Babies scream, couples stroll hand-in-hand and the air is filled with pop music, wild laughter and loud voices.

Usually, I wouldn't be seen *dead* here with my mum, but right now all I care about is finding The Dress.

After a long couple of hours, and just as I'm about to give up hope, we traipse into the seventh store that day. My t-shirt clings to my back with sweat, my head throbs from exhaustion and my shoulders ache from being lumbered with bags full of streamers, balloons and confetti.

"Come on, Nonny. Let's go home. We can

look for your dress another time," my mum yawns, fumbling around in her bag. She pulls out a pair of sunglasses and puts them on. She's ready to go.

"No, please!" I fret. "I'll find it soon, I promise. I just need to check a couple more shops, that's all!"

"Nonny, I'm tired. And your dad wants to go out, so we need to get back soon for Isaac."

"Can't he wait? If we leave now, you won't want to come back next time. Please… just two more stores," I moan.

"Don't you start whining, or I'll leave you here and you can make your own way home," my mum threatens.

I don't say another word. I'm about to give in and reluctantly follow her out, when I see it.

It's like it's calling me. I drop the bags I'm holding and throw my hands over my gaping mouth. It's *the* dress. Okay, so it's not the exact dress I'm wearing in my daydreams… but it's close. I make a beeline for it, not noticing who's in my way or even caring in the slightest. I NEED to get to it before anyone else does.

EEEEK – I love it! It's pastel pink and *smothered* in glitter so that it shimmers under the store's bright lights. It has long, loose sleeves and a flowery skirt that will *definitely* swish and sway when I move, which is exactly what I want.

"Mum, I've found what I want to wear!" I call, beckoning her over.

My mum picks up the bags I abandoned (whoops!) and ambles over, pushing her sunglasses to the top of her head. I wait with bated breath as she inspects the dress. She tilts her head, studying it carefully.

"Hmmm," she says, squinting her eyes and pursing her ruby-red lips.

She holds the corner of the dress between

her thumb and forefinger and turns it this way and that way… then this way again.

I wait.

"Hmmm," she repeats.

Come on, mum!

"Well…?" I prod, leaning forward to read her expression.

"This material is cheap."

I roll my eyes. "I really like it, mum. *Pleeease!*"

She sniffs, clears her throat, then eventually nods. YESSS – she approves! I squeal and wrap my arms around her.

"Let's go, then," she sighs.

She's been waiting for this moment almost as long as me. Now we *finally* get to go home.

I don't even need to try the dress on; I can already tell it will fit me perfectly. The rosy-cheeked girl at the till delicately folds my new dress, wraps it in gold tissue paper and carefully slips it into a gold bag. "This is such a pretty dress. It's been selling fast!" she says, handing me the bag.

That's just the confirmation I needed. "Thanks, I love it!"

"Is it for a special occasion?"

"Yep, my thirteenth birthday party!"

She raises her eyebrows. "Oooh, this is definitely the perfect dress for that. Happy birthday."

"Thank you," I smile.

It's official. The dress is mine!

When we get home, I tear up the stairs two at a time and race into my room. There's a knock at my door; I can tell it's Isaac by the faint sound his tiny fist makes.

"Come in, Isaac!" I call.

He enters my room in a green t-shirt and denim dungarees, and I immediately sweep him up into a cheerful cuddle.

"Guess what, Isaac?"

"What?" he asks, resting his head on my shoulder.

"I've got a new dress!" I grin, swinging the gold bag in front of him. "Look!"

"Woooow! It's gold!" he gasps, leaning forward to touch it.

"And my dress is pink! I'm gonna look just like a princess!"

"A pink princess!"

Isaac clambers out of my arms and onto my bed. I plonk beside him and we both fix our eyes on the gold bag in my hand.

I hold my breath as I gently pull the wrapped dress onto my lap. The gold paper makes it look like it's fit for royalty. I don't even *want* to unwrap it. But when I eventually do, I hold it up against me in the mirror and I'm transported to the night of my party – posing in the photo booth, dancing to my playlist, laughing with Daniel. I so desperately want to try it on, but wearing it for the first time next Saturday will make it EXTRA special.

I hang it up in my wardrobe and gaze at it like the proud winner of a new, shiny trophy at an award ceremony.

Just *wait* until tomorrow – I'm going to feel like a true SUPERSTAR when I get my hair braided for the first time. I can't wait.

I wake up on Sunday in the best mood EVER! Today's the day I transform into the princess I've been picturing in my dreams. In the garden, I grab Isaac off his tricycle and chuck him up in the air (I keep forgetting how heavy he is!) until he giggles and screams with delight. And I sing even LOUDER in the shower, much to my dad's distress.

"KEEP IT DOWN, NONNY!" he bellows as he bangs on the door.

I snigger to myself. Usually, I do exactly what he says so I won't get in any more trouble. But today, I wait until I hear his bedroom door slam shut, then carry on belting out my favourite song like I'm on-stage at my very own sold-out show.

Nothing is going to bring me down today.

My mum and I get to the salon at ten o'clock. It's surprisingly busy for a Sunday morning. Two women are already getting their hair done, chatting and laughing away.

One of the hairdressers peers at us over her glasses when we enter. She doesn't smile. And her face is stern, like a headteacher's. *Great.* My mum opens her mouth to speak, but The Scary Hairdresser gets in first.

"Take a seat; I won't be long," she commands in a strong Jamaican accent, pointing to two chairs in the corner.

We do as we're told. I shuffle closely behind my mum like a scared toddler, suddenly feeling very anxious. Does Nyah feel this intimidated when *she* comes to the hair salon?

As we sit down, I pick up a familiar scent in the air that instantly calms me down. It's a mixture of coconut and honey and all the special oils my mum uses every day. I loosen up a little and pick up an ancient magazine that's curling at the edges. Its pages are yellow-stained so I sift through it gingerly, patiently waiting my turn.

A chubby woman emerges from a room at the back of the salon, chomping noisily on a piece of gum. She's got a colourful scarf wrapped around her head and her flip-flops slap the floor as she marches over to grab the broom. I smile at her but she looks right through me like I'm invisible.

Why does no one smile around here?

An old film blasts from the TV. The hairdressers watch it while they work, howling with laughter every few minutes as if I'm not here, waiting. I pull out my phone to check the time. 10:47am. *Argh.* I'm starting to get VERY restless.

I can tell that my mum is feeling tense, too. Her back is as straight as a soldier's and she's constantly checking her watch, muttering things under her breath. *Humph!* Funny how parents work – she's super quick to scold me when *I'm* not on time, but I know she won't say a word now.

Just the other day, I was running late for school because I had been up past midnight nattering with Georgia on the phone. When I heard my mum's footsteps marching up the stairs, I froze, quivering with fear.

"NONNY!" she had screamed, bursting into my room.

"W-what?" The sock I was putting on dangled from my foot.

"What are you STILL doing here?"

"I'm leaving now, I promise," I gulped, pulling up the sock.

"You better be! I swear, if you were up all night on that phone of yours...!"

"I wasn't!" I fibbed. "I just woke up late, that's all!"

"And when I'm late to buy all the food for your beloved party, what then?"

"Muuum!"

"Clean your room as soon as you get home!" she bristled. Then she left.

I sigh loudly.

At quarter past eleven, The Scary Hairdresser calls me over. *Finally.* I take a deep breath as I watch her grab a comb from the drawer. Now I'm *really* scared. My tight curls tangle easily and they NEVER sit how I want them to, so raking a comb through them is like torture sometimes! And now, this terrifying woman with a scowl on her face is gripping the sharp-toothed comb and *staring* at me. I'm preparing myself for the worst, but the worst is even WORSE than I imagined.

She yanks at my hair so aggressively that my neck is close to snapping clean off my shoulders.

"Keep still," she orders.

I feel dizzy. Every strand of my hair feels like it's being ripped out from the root. I squeeze my eyes shut and press my lips together until they're numb.

"So, it's your birthday next week?"

Nod.

"Your first time getting braids?"

Nod.

I can't even speak. She must think I'm so weird.

Why didn't Nyah warn me that getting my hair done would be this painful? I clench my fists to hold back my sobs, but they escape anyway. I SO regret begging my mum to bring me here.

Six horrific hours later, my face is stained with tears and my scalp is red raw. I can barely look in the mirror once the ordeal is over, but I must admit that I *love* what I see.

And so do Georgia and Nyah! They

SCREAM when they see me the next day –
so loud that my eardrums are throbbing for
minutes afterwards.

"Wow, wow, wow! Nonny, you look
AMAZING!" Georgia gasps.

"We're like twins now! I LOVE it, Nonny!"
Nyah exclaims.

Hopefully Daniel will love it, too.

By Friday night, the day before my birthday
and PARTY OF THE YEAR, I can finally rest
my head on my pillow without wincing in pain.
I knew sitting through that *torture* would be
worth it eventually.

I lay under the covers and fizz with
excitement, nerves – the works! I could explode
with happiness. I call Nyah.

"Hey, Nonny."

"Hey, Nyah. I'm so excited for tomorrow!" I
bleat.

"Oh my gosh, me too! I can't *wait* to see what you're wearing."

"I can't wait for you to see it either. I think you'll really like it."

"I know I will! But do you know what I'm even *more* excited for?"

"What?"

"The photo booth! Everyone's gonna go crazy when they see that! I don't think anyone's *ever* had that at one of their parties before, not even Demi Baker!"

"Demi Baker hasn't had a photo booth at her party? But she's so rich!"

"I know, so she's gonna be so jealous! Anyway, Nonny, I need to sleep now. When we wake up, it'll be your birthday!"

"I know, I can't wait! Good night, Nyah."

"Good night."

I hang up and cocoon myself in my duvet.

Tomorrow is The Big Day – and it's going to be a day I'll NEVER forget.

COUNTDOWN TO MY PARTY: 19 HOURS

Ahhhh, the bliss of waking up on your birthday. Nothing can compare.

But waking up on the day of your first ever *party?* Even better. Time to blow up the balloons and shower the living room in confetti. It's party time!

I look out the window and all I see is pure, bright blue. I smile so wide my cheeks hurt. Perfect weather for what's about to be a *perfect* day.

I slide down the bannister, catching a whiff of my birthday breakfast. *Mmmm*, warm pancakes and fresh strawberries. I push open the kitchen door and I'm welcomed by two giant pink balloons. Numbers one and three. EEEEK – I'm thirteen today!

"Happy birthday to you, happy birthday to you, happy birthday dear Nonny, happy birthday to you!" my parents sing, enveloping me in a big hug. My dad's fuzzy beard roughly grazes my cheek, but I don't care. I look up at him to witness him actually *smiling* for once. Wow!

Isaac waddles towards me and grabs my hand. "Happy birthday, Nonny," he mumbles, clutching a pancake with his other hand.

I crouch down beside him and smack a big kiss on his cheek. "Thank you, Isaac!" I look up at my parents, smiling joyfully. "Thank you, mum. Thank you, dad!"

"Breakfast time, birthday girl," my dad

chirps, pulling out my chair for me.

Wow… he's never done *that* before! He pretends to curtsy, almost tripping up over his own slippers. I laugh and sit down, feeling on top of the world, and drizzle golden syrup all over my stack of pancakes before I tuck in.

"*YUMMM!* This is delicious!" I exclaim, my mouth full of pancakes.

"Eat with your mouth *closed*, Nonny," my mum warns, tutting.

"Sorry."

"So, are you excited for your party?"

"I'm so excited. And so are my friends."

"Just make sure you all behave, please. I don't want anything to get broken or stolen."

"My friends aren't like that, mum!"

"Well, you never know. I hear all these stories."

"Yeah, well, that won't happen, so don't worry."

"It better not. Otherwise nobody will step foot in this house again. Do you hear me?"

She refills my glass with orange juice. I stop chewing and stare at her in utter shock. What she *said* is normal, but what she *did* is baffling! On an ordinary day, even if I put on my sweetest, most innocent voice and ask her to get me something from the fridge, she'll bark,

"Stop being lazy and get it yourself!"

But it's not an ordinary day; it's my BIRTHDAY! So, I guess that's why my parents are treating me like a princess. Hmmm, I wonder how long this will last. Hopefully until tomorrow!

"Once you've finished your breakfast, get on with your chores," my dad orders.

Sigh. Maybe not.

I nod, not letting myself feel upset in the slightest. I refuse to be sad on my Big Day! I *even* load everything into the dishwasher after I devour every last crumb on my plate.

"Okay, off you go," my mum says, shooing me away. "Make sure you clean *properly*. We can't have your friends thinking that you come from a dirty household."

"I *know*, mum," I sigh, digging my nails into the palms of my hands to block the famous "I *Know*, Mum" eye-roll from escaping. *Don't do it,*

Nonny. It's not too late for her to cancel your party!
I grab the cleaning products from the cupboard and leave the kitchen.

"From top to bottom!" my dad calls after me.

The "I *Know*, Dad" eye-roll wastes no time.

I dust every corner of the house and polish every surface until it squeaks. I vacuum the living room from wall to wall, not daring to miss a spot. Usually, I zip around in a flash so I can relax as soon as possible. But not today! I must admit, the living room is the worst room in the house. My dad is *convinced* that he's an interior designer and has filled it with dull brown rugs and ugly beige sofas. *Gross.* I can't wait to see how *alive* it looks when it's packed with colourful decorations and people!

Even though I've spent most of my birthday cleaning, it doesn't matter. Because in just a few hours, my party will be in full swing, and I'll be eating all my favourite food and enjoying myself with all my friends. And Daniel will be here! Nothing can top that.

Sunlight streams through my window while I get ready. My lips clamp together in concentration as I apply my mascara. I'm NEVER allowed to wear makeup, but today, I'm a teenager! And that's what teenagers do. (Plus, my mum said I could.)

The sudden clattering from downstairs makes me jump so hard I nearly poke myself in the eye with the mascara wand. I sigh. It's my mum. Whenever there's a loud CRASH or BANG echoing through the walls of our house, it's either because she's rushing around, fed up or just plain angry. Today, it's probably all three. The DJ was late, and she's *still* waiting on the photo booth.

"It's not good enough that you're stuck in traffic. You should have left earlier!" I hear her blare into the phone.

When she gets like this, the whole family knows to stay well out of her way. My dad is in the garden with Isaac and I don't blame him! I'm happy to be in my room, making myself look pretty for my party. The only loud noise I want to hear right now is my music, so I crank it up to drown out the drama.

I add pink clips to my braids and cover my lips in layers and layers of cherry-flavoured gloss. My lips are so shiny they could rival Becky's! *Ugh* – not that I want to be *anything* like her. I shake my head to remove that disturbing thought from my mind and pack my makeup away.

The time has come to put on... *The Dress*.

I haven't laid a finger on it since I placed it in my wardrobe like it was a precious diamond, too scared that touching it will jinx EVERYTHING! But now I have to. I handle the sacred gown and slip into it as carefully as I

can, suddenly feeling quite nervous. *Why didn't
I try it on in the store? What if it looks terrible?
What if Daniel doesn't like it?!*

Mini gymnasts flip and tumble in my
stomach as I tread towards the mirror. I
squeeze my eyes shut as my heart tries to
escape from my chest. It's time!

"Three… two… one," I whisper, slowly
opening my eyes for the grand reveal.

I gasp as I stare at my reflection. Wow! I look
GREAT.

Am I allowed to say that?

I bat my eyelashes, put my hand on my hip and pout like a superstar posing for the paparazzi.

I look like a different Nonny. I *feel* like a different Nonny. Not the twelve-year-old daydreamer who drags herself to school every day and isn't allowed outside of her house after four o'clock. Today, I'm a carefree, excited, *mature* teenager who can do what she wants! *Well…* if my parents let me, of course.

I spot my shoebox of stones in the mirror's reflection. Just before I got into bed last night, I was super nervous and needed all the comfort I could get. I hauled the box out from under my bed and rummaged around for my Magic Stone. It's charcoal in colour, smooth as marble, and has this perfect, white line that runs ALL the way around it, like it was etched by an artist. I call it my Magic Stone because every single time I hold it, I instantly feel better. It's *never* let me down before, and it didn't last night either. When I found it, I held it close to my chest, wishing that today would be PERFECT.

But now that I'm a teenager, it might be time to keep my stones stashed away for good. Not even my besties know I keep them, and The Witches would fry me in their cauldron if they ever found out! I walk over to the shoebox, hug it lovingly, and then push it even further under my bed.

I return to the mirror and spin round and round, overjoyed and overexcited. When my dizziness settles, I open my door and peek my head through the gap, trying to listen to what's going on. I hear voices. I think the photo booth is here!

"Right here is fine! No, no, to the left a little," my mum commands.

"Here?"

"No, more to the right."

I imagine a tubby, sweaty man in a grimy vest and jeans, panting like a dog, while my mum watches him struggle.

"Here?"

"That will have to do, I suppose," she huffs.

"Alright. Enjoy taking photos. We'll be back tomorrow."

WOOHOO! It *is* the photo booth! I sprint downstairs to finally see my dream party in real life.

I push open the living room door and my jaw drops in awe. It's just like stepping into my very own fantasy world!

The first thing I see? MY DREAM CAKE! It graces the table in the centre of the room, taking up space with all its scrumptiousness. It's a three-tier, out-of-this-world, melt-in-the-mouth masterpiece. The bottom tier is lemon sponge cake, filled with tangy lemon curd and buttercream. The middle is red velvet cake, coated in thick white chocolate frosting. And to top it off, my all-time favourite – *salted caramel!* There are only two candles; numbers one and three, just like my birthday breakfast balloons. And they're PINK! My mouth waters as I stare lovingly at my three favourite cakes combined into one, just like I've always wanted. It's a dream come true!

The rest of the food on the table looks like we're getting ready for a royal banquet! Okay, so maybe the Royal Family don't stuff their faces with cheese and onion crisps and double chocolate brownies – but this spread is perfect for a *birthday* queen, at least.

There's sandwiches cut into triangles, pepperoni pizza, BBQ chicken wings, and cupcakes topped with swirly pink and purple icing. Melted chocolate flows from the fountain like a mini waterfall (*mmmm, just imagine a real-life chocolate waterfall!*), and juicy strawberries and grapes are laid out on the plates beneath it.

I see: sugary donuts; donuts covered in sprinkles; donuts bursting with raspberry jam; marshmallows on sticks; bags of pastel-pink candy floss; and endless bowls of sour sweets. The table is overflowing with so many treats it looks like it might collapse! I'm ecstatic. I have to stop myself from reaching out and shoving all this glorious food down my throat.

I look around in fascination, my mouth open so wide I could catch flies. The living room has transformed from its dull brown and beige to my pink and purple party paradise! The whole place is decked out with glittery pink and purple balloons. Lilac streamers hang from the ceiling and pink confetti is strewn around the room like sprinkles on a cake. The photo booth gleaming in the corner is the cherry on top. If only The Witches could see me now! This is *far* from a party for losers.

I look at my phone, hoping that my besties get here soon. It's five o'clock. EEEEK – they'll be here any minute now. And I feel terrible saying it, but I'm even *more* excited for Daniel to arrive! He'll be *so* impressed by the decorations, the food, the CAKE. I just hope he loves my dress, too.

The doorbell rings. *AAAAHHH!* I skid across the hallway and bolt to the door to greet my BFFs.

"HAPPY BIRTHDAY, NONNY!" they scream, as I swing the door open.

"Thank you!"

"You look *fantastic!* Like a famous singer! No, actually, like a *model!*" Georgia gasps. She's in a white t-shirt and pink pinafore. *And* she's wearing pink eyeshadow, just like the girls we watch and envy online. Her curls bounce as she walks into the house, and her honey-toned skin glows in the sunshine.

"Yeah, Nonny, you look amazing!" Nyah grins.

She's wearing a white frilly blouse with puffy sleeves and a short denim skirt. Pink and purple thread is entwined with her dark braids, and gold jewellery (probably from her mum's stash) decorates her wrists.

"So do you guys!" I squeal, hugging my best friends tightly.

They hand me my present. It's perfectly wrapped (Nyah *definitely* did it!) in glossy silver paper. *I wonder what it could be!* Georgia and Nyah watch me eagerly as I rip my gift open, letting the wrapping paper drop to the floor (I must remember to pick it up before my mum yells at me). When my gift is finally revealed, I see that it's a book. But it's not the type of book that you borrow from the library. It's a

friendship book! And it's PINK! My lower lip
trembles. The front cover is emblazoned with
'BEST FRIENDS FOREVER' in a magenta felt-
tip pen, just above a photo of me and my BFFs
at the park. Underneath, it says, 'WE LOVE
YOU NONNY'. I blink back tears as I thumb
through pages of photos and sweet messages
from the two bestest friends in the whole
world.

"*Wow,*" I breathe. "I LOVE it! Thank you so
much!"

"Yay! I knew you would! Nyah wanted to
make us all friendship bracelets at first, but I
knew I'd lose mine. So, we made this instead!"
Georgia confesses.

"It's the best present EVER!" I exclaim.

We race to my room and I delicately place
my new friendship book in my bedside drawer.
Then, we spend the next half an hour dancing,
taking silly videos and snapping pictures like

we're in a girl band. It's so much fun!

When we're all danced out and slightly out of breath, Georgia wanders over to the mirror.

"Ugh, I look so fat," she frowns, turning her body to inspect it from all angles.

"No, you DON'T, Georgia!" I gasp. "You look fabulous!"

"Yeah, Georgia. You really do!" Nyah agrees, putting her phone away to focus on Georgia's troubles.

"I look *fat*. This dress shouldn't be this tight," she wails.

Georgia is always moaning about her weight, forever pulling on her tummy like it's playdough. Nyah and I try to make her feel better all the time, telling her that she's BEAUTIFUL no matter what size she is.

"Don't be silly, Georgia! Besides, I bet *you* didn't stuff your face with six pancakes this morning!" I cross my eyes and puff my cheeks out, trying to make her laugh. But she doesn't.

"You *can* do that, though. You're not fat!"

"And neither are you!" I cry, feeling bad for her.

I *am* surprisingly quite slim, considering all that I eat. I *love* to eat – especially all the junk food my mum hides at the back of the cupboard. She thinks I don't know about the hordes of crisps, chocolate bars and biscuits she hides in there once she's been shopping, that she says can only come out on special occasions (like TODAY!). Little does she know, I'm a Professional Midnight Snacker.

"Stop it, Georgia! You look brilliant," Nyah says.

"Whatever."

"You always look good, Georgia," I smile. She never believes us, but we'll never stop telling her. "Now, cheer up!"

"Thanks, guys," she sighs. "I will."

Nyah and I join Georgia by the mirror and embrace her in a tight hug. I'm happy that she feels better, but her mini meltdown has now rubbed off on *me!* We were having such fun, but time is ticking, and I'm starting to get worried. I slouch onto my bed and start picking at my eyelashes. I'm suddenly a nervous wreck.

"Stop it, Nonny! You're ruining your makeup!" Georgia shrieks.

"What if no one shows up?" I whimper. "What if it's just us?"

"Of *course* people will show up, Nonny. Why would anyone want to miss a *party?*" Nyah dismisses my fears, joining me on the bed and putting her arm around my shoulder.

"Because they don't like me!"

"That's stupid! You're just getting nervous, that's all. Stop pulling on your eyelashes like that, too. It's freaking me out!" Georgia cries, covering her eyes.

"Sorry," I say, sitting on my hands.

"I bet people will start showing up any minute. And even if they don't, we'll still have fun like we always do."

"But what would be the point?" I groan. "Have you *seen* how much food is downstairs? If no one turns up, my parents will *kill* me for wasting all their money!"

"I could eat all that food *easily*," Georgia boasts. "Anyway, you're worrying too much. It's your birthday today; you're supposed to be happy."

"Yeah, please cheer up, Nonny. We don't want to see you sad. You're thirteen today – you've been looking forward to this for *ages!*"

"I know," I mumble. "I'm trying. It's just – I want people to show up *now*, that's all."

"Nonny, it's not even six yet! You're stressing *me* out," Georgia chuckles, rolling her eyes jokingly.

"Yeah, we've still got ages. And remember, people always show up late to parties. Even *you* did it when I had my party two years ago!"

I laugh, remembering the time I was an hour late to Nyah's pyjama party. It wasn't my fault though; my dad was supposed to give me a lift, but he'd fallen asleep on the sofa, snoring like a wild boar, and I couldn't wake him up for ages!

"True."

"Sooo, are you gonna calm down now? Am I allowed to have some of the food, by the way? I'm starving." Georgia rubs her stomach.

Nyah giggles. "You have to wait, Georgia! Even though I kind of want some, too."

"Can we, Nonny?"

"My mum said we have to wait, sorry."

Georgia sighs dramatically and flops down on the bed. "*Fiiiine.* But cheer up now, please. No more worrying!"

I take a deep breath. "Sorry. I'll stop now, I

promise!"

My friends are right. There's no point worrying. Well, not in front of them, anyway.

I walk downstairs and perch on the bottom step, drumming my fingers along the bannister. I glance up at the clock. It's 5:57pm. No one's here yet.

The music from the DJ is as loud as I'd hoped it would be, but I just want it to STOP! It's giving me a banging headache and I can't think straight. Georgia and Nyah are upstairs giggling at our funny photos without a care in the world. Lucky them. *They* don't have to worry about no one showing up to their thirteenth birthday party, or stress about the fact that their parents have gone to so much effort just to have it completely wasted.

Chioma from Maths is *always* on time; why is *she* not here yet? And I at least expected James and Mike from French to be here by now, too.

My hand automatically reaches for my eyelashes, ready to pull at them again, but I quickly realise and stop myself. *Aaah,* I wish I hadn't scoffed that stack of pancakes for breakfast; they're going to make a reappearance any minute now.

Just imagine if no one shows up! And if they do, what if it's the worst party they've ever been to? Emotions bubble away inside me like a boiling kettle. But just as I'm about to spill over... the doorbell rings.

I jump up, ecstatic.

"MUM!" I yelp.

Even though I'm *thirteen* today, she still won't let me open the door by myself – except to Georgia and Nyah. I watch eagerly as she does the honours, wiping my sweaty palms on the skirt of my dress.

Relief rushes over me. Chioma, Rachel and Grace bundle through the front door, each holding a gift bag for me. *For me!* They hug me one by one.

"Happy birthday, Nonny!"

"Wow, you look so nice!"

"Hope you like your present!"

It feels like my dreams are finally coming true. The first guests have arrived!

"GEORGIA, NYAH!" I yell up the stairs.

My mum takes their presents and leads them to the living room while I take a deep breath and smile to myself. Everything is going to be just fine.

My BFFs bound down the stairs.

"Are people here?" Nyah asks, excited.

"Yeah! Let's go to the living room!"

"WOOHOO!" Georgia hoots.

We skip into the living room. It's finally time to get this party started.

Before I know it, the room is crowded with

happy people and wrapped presents, and my worries are floating in the air like my giant balloons. I've never been the centre of attention before and I've never cared to be. But today, I'm *loving* it. Don't tell anyone, but I could get used to this.

We're an hour in, and my party is just how I pictured it in my daydreams, but BETTER.

"This is such a good party, Nonny!"

"I'm having SO MUCH FUN!"

"You should have parties all the time, Nonny!"

There's a queue for the photo booth, the food is going down a treat, and my playlist is bouncing through the sound system like we're at a concert. Most importantly, everyone is having FUN!

I feel like the most popular girl in school, like the ones in my favourite American TV shows. I think I might *really* be throwing the party of the YEAR!

I'm dancing on cloud nine. I look around the room to take in all the laughter and smile at the jolly faces here to celebrate with me.

But then it hits me.

Where's Daniel?

I look down at my phone, wishing a text from him would magically appear (which would be *insane* because he doesn't have my number – although I really, really wish he did). He *said* he was coming, so why is he so late?

When I look up, I notice a black car cruising into our driveway. EEEEK! I run out into the hallway.

"*Muuuum*, someone's here!" I yell towards the kitchen.

When she reaches the door, I peer nervously over her shoulder as the car comes to a stop.

It's *Daniel!*

I scoot back to the stairs, pretending to be

cool and calm, as though I haven't been waiting for him to walk through the door since the moment my party started.

Suddenly, my mouth is dry and my palms are moist. He came! *He actually came!*

Footsteps approach the door.

Gulp.

I hiss at my mum to open it before the bell rings. As she twists the door handle to reveal the love of my life, my grin stretches so wide it almost hurts.

But when the door finally opens and I see who's standing on my doorstep, my heart plunges into my stomach. There in the doorway, all dressed up and beaming brightly at my mum, is *not* the person I expected. It's *not* Dreamy Daniel.

It's my worst nightmare.

5

"Happy birthday, Nonny," The Witches croon, wearing the fakest, most sickly sweet smiles I've EVER seen.

I'm speechless. I can't even open my mouth to respond. I blink fast, suddenly feeling very sick. My mum smiles back at The Most Evil Girls In The World.

"Thanks, girls. The party's just through there."

Nooooooo! I can't let her fall for their tricks!

"Thank you," they sing.

Why are they here? What do they want?

They saunter past me, looking as smug as can be. Amber subtly knocks my shoulder with hers. I scowl at her, my blood boiling so ferociously I could explode.

"Nonny, don't be rude," my mum hisses through gritted teeth, nodding in the direction of The Witches as they disappear into the living room. Georgia and Nyah are going to faint in shock when they see them.

"Mum, I *hate* them. I didn't even invite them! Please make them leave," I wail, leaning hopelessly against the bannister.

My mum bends down so that she's staring at me dead in the eye.

"You don't hate anyone. They're nice girls who've come here to celebrate your birthday, so I will *not* make them leave."

I can't believe it! She is well and truly under

The Witches' spell!

My eyes fill with angry tears.

"*Muuuum!* You don't understand–"

"What I DO understand is that you're acting like a spoilt brat. Now get in there and enjoy the party that me and your dad have spent a lot of time and money on."

I look down at my shoes in shame.

I don't even have the energy to argue. My mum straightens up, gives me a nudge and watches me trudge back into the party that I had been excited about for so long. Now all I want is for it to be over.

I never thought in a million years that this would happen. I watched The Witches trample on one of my invitations before my very eyes. They told me that only losers were invited to my party. They *hate* me and my friends. Why would they want to show up?

Ugh – to wreak havoc, that's why!

As soon as I step foot back inside, Georgia and Nyah dash over to me, their faces like thunder.

"What the heck are The Witches doing here, Nonny?"

Don't cry, Nonny. Don't. Cry.

"Nonny, why did you let them in?"

Too late.

The tears start streaming. My besties quickly shove me out the living room and lead me to the bathroom.

"M-my m-mum let them i-in," I gulp in between sobs, my shoulders heaving as I slump onto the toilet lid.

Nyah grabs a bundle of toilet paper and dabs at my eyes and cheeks. "You're ruining your makeup, Nonny. Stop crying."

Georgia's brow furrows. "We need to make sure they leave!"

"How are we gonna do that?!" I screech, my

eyesight blurry with tears.

Georgia shrugs helplessly. "I don't know."

"We're not going to do anything. They're just jealous that they weren't invited. They'll probably get bored soon and leave, anyway," Nyah says.

Georgia nods aggressively in agreement. "Yeah, she's right. You're not gonna let *The Witches* spoil your birthday! None of us are. Are we?"

I shake my head and smile weakly. They're right. I've been looking forward to this day for *so long*. There's no way The Witches are going to ruin my thirteenth birthday.

"No," I sniff. "Thanks, guys."

"Cool! Now let's go." Nyah pulls her phone out of her pocket. She beams. "I'm getting so many views on my videos. Oh my gosh, and Michael commented on my picture!"

Georgia and I glance at each other and roll

our eyes.

I get up and check the mirror before we re-enter the wild. My mascara has run and smudged so I look like a panda.

"Nooo! Look at my eyes!" I whine.

"Don't worry, I'll help you," Georgia reassures me, wetting a sheet of toilet paper and gently wiping the black splotches from under my eyes.

"Thanks, Georgia," I smile, admiring my reflection. I look normal again!

"What do you think, Nyah?"

"Mmmm," Nyah says, without lifting her head to check.

Georgia sighs and grabs my hand. She marches me out, Nyah following closely behind, and we both take a deep breath before we step back inside the living room.

The Witches are the first people we see. Amber is dressed in a hot-pink skirt and cream crop top. Her hair is in the neatest French plaits I've ever seen and she's doused herself in a strawberry-scented fragrance. Becky's wearing a white velvet halter-neck top and jeans, and of course, her signature lip gloss.

Amber smirks when we make eye contact and strides up to me, Becky rushing behind her.

"Have you been *crying?*" she jeers, elbowing Becky, who's busy brushing crumbs from her lips.

Her head jerks up to attention and she screeches with laughter when she looks at me.

"Oh my gosh, what a *baby*. You look a mess," Becky scoffs, her mouth full of crisps.

I part my lips to reply but my fantastic BFF, Georgia, jumps in to save me.

"And you look like you're trying too hard, *as usual!*"

"Shut up, fatty."

Georgia's face reddens and her eyes travel to the carpet, where they stay for the rest of the conversation.

"Why have you made such an effort for a party that only *losers* are invited to?" Nyah snorts, crossing her arms across her chest and looking The Witches up and down.

"This is nothing. I would wear this to the *shop*," Amber snaps. She looks around at the balloons and streamers with disgust. "This is the most boring party I've ever been to."

"Good thing you weren't invited, then," I bark.

My heart is pounding with fear but I'm proud of myself for standing my ground.

Becky steps a little closer so that I catch a whiff of the cheese and onion crisps she just wolfed down. *Gross.*

"Well, we're here now, so you better *hope* we

enjoy ourselves. Or we're gonna tell everyone that this was the worst party *ever*."

Nyah steps forward to be face-to-face with Becky. I know she's scared, but she doesn't show it. "Or you can just leave."

"We're not going anywhere," Amber smiles, twirling one of her plaits around her index finger.

"Let's just go, guys," Georgia mumbles.

I don't want to, but I know we've been defeated. We turn around and skulk off, leaving The Witches standing tall like champions. We may have stood up for ourselves, but we all feel worse than we did before the argument. The music pumps, people dance, but we sit down in a huddle, away from the party.

"Well, we tried," Nyah huffs.

She grabs a pink paper bowl filled to the brim with *extra sour* jelly sweets.

I know what's coming next.

It's a tradition at our sleepovers; we each take a handful of sweets and stuff them in our mouths. The first person to spit them out loses and HAS to do a dare.

It's a great way to cheer us up right now, so I grin and scoop up my handful. I pass the bowl to Georgia, but she shakes her head and lightly pushes it away. Usually, she's the first to want to play, so I know that Becky's words about her size have got to her. I put my arm around her and pull her closer to me.

"Georgia, you know you're not fat. You do know that, right?"

"Yeah, George, don't listen to them. They're both stupid."

"Exactly. And did you *smell* Becky's breath?" I whisper, pinching my nose.

Georgia manages a small smile and reaches for her portion of sweets.

This is why I love my friends. We always get

back up when we're beaten down. Despite The Witches crashing my special day and upsetting us like this, I'm finally starting to think that everything's going to be okay again.

But I'm wrong.

Because in that moment, while me and my besties sit together in the corner of my living room, something DREADFUL happens. Nyah's eyes widen in horror as she points to the other end of the room. Her sweets tumble to the floor.

Then, she screams.

Have you ever seen something happen in slow motion before?

I hadn't – until now.

The music pulsing from the speakers suddenly sounds like it's gurgling deep beneath the ocean. My friends' mouths open wide. Their arms reach out.

But it's too late.

It feels like I'm wading through clay, trying to get to my tumbling cake before it collides with the carpet.

Then I come back to reality, just as my dream cake lands in a messy heap with an almighty THUD. All three tiers of it.

"NOOOOO!" I scream.

I drop to my knees with my head in my hands. I hear sniggers and hushed whispers.

"What is she *doing*?"

"Oh my gosh, it's just a *cake*."

"Ermmm… this is weird."

Nyah tries to haul me to my feet by grabbing my hand, but I stay right where I am.

"Nonny, get up!" she hisses at me, peering over her shoulder at the people starting to gather around us. I can tell she's embarrassed.

"Leave me alone!" I grieve, looking around in despair.

My cake has *completely* fallen apart. Chunks of it are scattered across the carpet like pieces of a puzzle.

The music is still thumping as if nothing has happened. It feels like the soundtrack to a tragic movie: **THE WORST PARTY IN HISTORY: STARRING NONNY.**

The Witches stand beside the table where my beautiful cake once stood, giggling behind their hands. Then, Amber folds her arms smugly, looks right into my tear-filled eyes, and mouths, *"Whoops."*

They're the culprits; they're the ones who pushed over my cake. I just KNOW IT!

I'm not a fighter at all; I can barely argue with my best friends, but something strange comes over me at that moment. I'm blinded by an unstoppable rage and I spring up and launch at Amber like a rocket, tugging one of her plaits so hard that it unravels. I feel frantic hands on me from all angles, trying to pull me back to my senses. Amber is screaming. Becky is pushing me. I can't make out the words she's saying, but she looks terrified of the hysterical lunatic before her.

I can just about hear Georgia yelp, "GET OFF HER, NONNY!" but I'm in a determined attack mode. I'm like an angry cat, clawing away at Amber's perfect face with venom in each scratch.

"I hate you! Why don't you just go home?!" I cry.

"Get OFF me, you FREAK!"

Without warning, Becky wallops me in the chest and I plummet backwards onto a spongey mattress of birthday cake.

Before I know it, crumbs decorate my hair and my princess dress is smothered in icing. I lay sprawled on the carpet, wailing in anguish, more heartbroken that I didn't get to taste my dream cake than the fact that I'm lying in it.

Any minute now, I'm certain a hidden camera crew are about to jump out of the shadows and shriek, "GOT YOU!!! YOU'RE BEING PRANKED!"

But... nothing.

Georgia and Nyah hoist me up by my arms and dab at my cake-covered braids and filthy dress with used napkins. I blub loudly while everyone else stands around awkwardly, avoiding eye contact with me. Some of them are even stifling giggles. The Witches are at the back of the crowd; Amber clutches her bleeding face while Becky comforts her. I can feel their eyes burning into me, but they're the least of my worries right now. I just *know* that my parents will never let me step foot outside of these four walls again, unless I'm going to school.

"Nonny, listen. I'm going to get your mum," Nyah insists.

She disappears upstairs, leaving me bawling in Georgia's arms.

"It's not that bad, Nonny," she says, stroking my back. "It's just a cake. And you can wash your dress. Everything else is still–"

"Just a *cake?*" I interrupt, extremely offended. "Wash my *dress?* How can you *say* that? You know how much I wanted this cake, Georgia! And just look at me!" I stare mournfully at the pretty dress I've been so in love with for ages, and a new set of hot tears spout from my eyes.

"I know, Nonny. It sucks. But you can still enjoy the rest of your party."

"*How?* Can't you see that they've ruined *everything?*"

I shoot The Witches an icy stare.

"I promise it will be fine. When your mum comes downstairs, we'll tell her that they pushed over the cake. Then they'll have no choice but to leave!"

I nod, praying she's right. Even though I feel slightly better, nothing can change the fact that my birthday bash is RUINED. To make matters worse, The Witches march over to us.

"You're gonna pay for this, you crazy weirdo!" Amber spits, her face bright red.

Georgia leaps to my defence. "Leave her alone, Amber. You started this. We know you pushed over that cake!"

"I did no such thing," Amber retorts, folding her arms and jutting out her chin.

"We know you did, you liar. And I'm gonna tell Nonny's mum that, too."

"Of course *you'd* be the most upset about the cake, fatty. You probably would have gobbled it up all by yourself!"

"Shut up Amber, you horrible, evil little–" I start.

"NONNY!" my mum blares, stamping over to the DJ's set and wrenching the plug out of the socket.

The sudden silence buzzes in my ears.

"Hey!" the DJ hollers, confused.

No one acknowledges him.

My mum gawks at Amber's bloody face, then at me covered in cake, then down at the soiled carpet.

She gasps in shock.

"THAT'S IT! Everybody out – now!"

Nobody moves. She takes a long, deep breath.

"NOWWWWW!!!" she roars, her mouth as wide as a black hole.

Her lungs must be on fire.

Suddenly, the crowd parts and everyone scurries frantically towards the door, petrified of the fuming dragon-mum standing before them. Even the DJ vanishes.

I shrink like a wilting flower; my mum's going to *kill* me once everyone has gone. At the same time, I'm ecstatic that this nightmare of a party is about to end. But just when I think the worst is over, Becky does the unthinkable.

She scrapes a huge piece of lemon cake from the carpet and lobs it straight at my HEAD! I shriek as lemon curd splatters across my face and just about misses my eye. My mum's eyes widen in horror as I seize the first thing I can reach and hurl it in Becky's direction.

"HEY!" she cries, clutching the side of her face as the donut I just threw bounces off it.

She's dressed from head to toe in sugar.

Hearing the commotion, floods of banished partygoers pour back into the room to see what all the fuss is about.

The next thing I know, someone shouts, "FOOD FIGHT!!!" And that's when all hell breaks loose.

Half-eaten sandwiches jet in all different directions, slices of pizza smack people in the face and mini cupcakes whoosh over people's heads. Everyone is hooting and shrieking with laughter. Even Georgia and Nyah are going for it. I might have been too, if this wasn't MY party being ruined, MY house being destroyed and MY life that will soon be cut short by two furious parents.

My mum is running around like a headless chicken, trying to get a room full of hyper twelve- and thirteen-year-olds to "PLEASE STOP!!!"

Just like the teachers at school, she has no luck. I watch her duck, dive and weave her way through the crowd to rush upstairs, yelling for my dad.

My life is well and truly over now.

I crouch down like I'm on the battlefield and crawl over to a quiet corner of the room, dodging flying chipolatas and chocolate brownies. I'm anxiously waiting for the moment my dad bursts through the door in a vicious rage. Any moment now. Any moment now. Any moment–

"WHAT IS GOING ON?" he bellows. He nearly smashes into the photo booth as he tears his way into the living room. He's wearing his wonky reading glasses and those awfully tattered, striped pyjamas with the hole in the knee, AND he's holding one of my mum's bedroom slippers above his head like a fluffy weapon. Not only am I *scared stiff,* but I'm also SO embarrassed.

What is he doing?!

He lunges at the first person he sees – Joe from History – and aims at him with the slipper. Joe screeches and bends down to avoid being hit, but my dad chases him out of the door.

"GET OUT NOW! GET OUT NOW! ALL OF YOU!"

People finally listen.

The Witches dump the food they're holding and scamper out the door after Joe, giggling breathlessly. The rest of the party soon follows, until it's just me, Georgia, Nyah and my mum left. I hear my dad yelling, girls screaming, boys laughing. The neighbours are going to think we're CRAZY! We run out to the hallway to watch my party guests bolt down the road into the sunset, trying to escape the bonkers man with the slipper in his hand.

"We're so sorry, Nonny," Nyah mutters, looking ashamed.

She and Georgia both look a SIGHT! The buttercream in Georgia's hair makes her curls stick together and Nyah's white top is soiled with raspberry jam. Both of their faces are spattered with chocolate, icing and other things that should NOT be on their faces.

It's almost funny.

But before I can even *think* about laughing,

my dad stomps back into the house and slams the door so hard the entire house shakes. Even my mum flinches.

My dad has red-hot fury in his eyes. I can almost see the flames dancing in his pupils and feel the steam blowing from his ears. He glares at me as he breathes heavily, like a bull about to charge. I'm frozen to the spot, waiting for him to bulldoze me down me with his horns.

"YOU WILL CLEAN THIS UP IMMEDIATELY!" he booms.

Spit flies from his mouth like oil sizzling in a pan, landing in his beard.

We all jump.

Even the paintings on the wall rattle from the vibration of his thunderous voice. Well, almost.

I am SO glad my besties are staying with me tonight.

"Yes, dad," I murmur, trembling with fear. "I'm really sorry."

I look at my mum, hoping she'll feel a teeny bit sorry for me.

"Get out of my sight," she seethes.

Her voice croaks from all the shouting she's done this evening.

I dart back to the living room without looking back, followed closely by Georgia and Nyah who both look like they've seen a ghost. Before I enter, I see Isaac standing at the top of the stairs in his pyjamas, rubbing his eyes with one hand and clinging onto his worn-out teddy bear with the other. Poor little Isaac; all the crazy noise must have shocked him awake. I wish I could wrap him up in a gigantic hug, but I need to get away from my enraged parents as quickly as possible.

"Sorry, Isaac," I mouth, feeling terribly guilty.

Georgia, Nyah and I duck into the living room, and I shut the door behind us. We slump onto the only clean sofa left, feeling helpless. I look around. The rest of the room looks like a bomb site. My cake, my *beautiful* dream cake, has been trampled into the carpet I carefully vacuumed just a few hours ago. Melted chocolate from the fountain I longed for has been splashed up and across the white walls. Sandwich fillings are smeared all over the table and chairs. The purple streamers lay ripped and hopeless on the floor, and confetti is wedged between the cushions on the sofas. Chicken bones have made their way into every nook and cranny of the living room like a treasure hunt.

Figuring out how to clean up this mess is going to be harder than my algebra homework.

"Are you sure we can stay tonight, Nonny?" Georgia whispers, biting her nails anxiously.

"Yeah, I think we should go home," Nyah gulps.

I start to panic.

"No, please stay. Please," I beg. "He'll calm down. Plus, if you guys go now, he will literally *kill* me."

There's a pause.

"Yeah… I guess…" Georgia ponders.

I clutch both of their arms in desperation. "Please stay. I promise I'll make it up to both of you."

My eyes well with tears. This is all so unfair.

First, the one person I *really* want to come to my party doesn't. Then, the two people I really *don't* want to come to my party do! The cake of my dreams is basically another carpet, the whole place is a complete and utter MESS, and now my parents *hate* me. Not only did they shout at my friends (which, along with my dad attacking everyone with my mum's slipper, has left me crippled with embarrassment), but they shouted at *me*. On my *birthday*.

Turning thirteen has been seriously eventful, but NOT in a good way.

Georgia and Nyah glance at each other and nod slowly.

"Okay," Nyah sighs.

I feel so relieved. At least *one* good thing has come out of this terrible day.

We grab rubber gloves, cleaning spray and old cloths, and get to it. As I scrub and polish every corner of the living room like Cinderella,

I think about Daniel. As it turns out, I'm kind of glad he didn't come in the end. He would have thought my parents and I were crackers, and he'd *never* want to talk to me again.

Not that he does now, anyway.

It's midnight by the time we finish cleaning. At least that means this dreadful day is officially over. I'm so thankful for my friends. If it wasn't for them, I'd probably be here until four in the morning. We whip off our gloves and wipe our brows. We're all drenched in sweat.

My stomach growls. "I'm so hungry. I wish there was cake left," I sigh.

"Me too," Georgia agrees. "Or some chicken wings. Or that pizza. It was *sooo* nice. And the donuts too. Oh my gosh – it was SO funny when you threw that donut at Becky's head, Nonny." She giggles.

"That was hilarious," Nyah chirps. "And I

can't believe you scratched Amber's face!"

I cover my face with my hands in shame. Not only am I heartbroken at the catastrophe my party turned out to be, but I'm SO embarrassed by my behaviour.

"*Argh,* I can't believe I did that."

"Who cares? She deserved it! She *definitely* pushed your cake over. I would have done the same thing as you," Georgia shrugs.

"Me too. You could tell she was SO scared when you came for her! It was like watching a wrestling match on TV. I wish I could watch it on repeat," Nyah laughs.

I find it in myself to chuckle along with my best friends. But it's not real laughter. I feel empty inside, and not just because I'm *starving*. When I said my birthday would be a day I'd never forget, I did NOT mean like this. If I knew how it would end, I would never have thrown this stupid party.

Nyah sighs and scrolls through her phone, admiring the selfies she posted online earlier.

"At least I posted good pictures before we looked like *this!*" She tugs at the collar of her blouse that was once a spotless white.

Georgia hurls her a suspicious look. "I hope you put good pictures up of *all* of us, not just yourself!"

"What do you mean? Of course I did! See!" Nyah retorts, shoving her phone in Georgia's face.

Georgia takes a quick look. "Humph! I'm surprised," she shrugs.

"Well, *I'm* surprised you even care. You always go on about how much you *hate* pictures."

"I do. Because you always post bad pictures of me!"

"What are you on about, Georgia? That's not true–"

They're too busy bickering to notice me slink out of the room. I head to the toilet and lock the door, then count to ten before I can bear to look in the mirror.

What I see shocks me.

What a state! My wonderful pink dress – *The Dress* – has a huge tear down the side and it's stained with cola and BBQ sauce. It's RUINED; I can never wear it again! Even if I try to keep it, my mum will make sure she chucks it away herself. The thought of her bundling it up in a black binbag and hurling it into the skip down the road breaks my heart in two. And if I thought my mascara was smudged earlier, I can't believe what it looks like now. There are specks of chocolate all over my face and my once-beautiful braids are peppered with sugar and crumbs.

What did I do to deserve this?

I've been such a good daughter and big sister

for WEEKS! I've done all my chores and my homework and come home straight from school without moaning. I've done everything my parents have asked of me for *sooo* long, but I'm *still* being punished.

Whatever – I just can't wait to have a nice, hot shower and get into bed.

When I join Georgia and Nyah again, they're sitting in silence. I guess they're all argued out.

"Come on, guys. Let's get ready for bed," I say, wearily.

We drag ourselves upstairs, hot and sticky after such a stressful evening. Once we shower and cram into my bed like sardines, I realise my throat is dry and my eyes are puffy from all the tears I shed earlier. I think I've cried enough for the entire year!

Georgia rubs my back. "You'll be okay, Nonny. Everyone will have forgotten about this by Monday. It will be like one big, distant memory," she smiles.

"Yeah, one hundred percent. And you'll be laughing about it all in a few weeks," Nyah assures me.

I don't believe them, but I say, "Thanks, guys. And thanks for staying with me tonight."

We share a three-way hug and I click off my bedside lamp. But just as I'm dozing off to forget about The Worst Day Of My Life, Nyah gasps loudly.

"*What?*" Georgia and I hiss impatiently.

I turn the lamp back on and stare at Nyah. The look on her face tells me she has some bad news. "Erm... Nonny..."

She hesitantly passes me her phone. I sit up in bed and grab it from her with shaking hands. Georgia looks over my shoulder. What we see makes my heart hurtle to my stomach.

It's a video of me. I'm on the floor with my head in my hands, knee-deep in cake crumbs and smeared buttercream. It's racked up A LOT of comments. I cover my mouth with my hand, shaking my head fiercely.

"Oh my gosh," Georgia exhales.

I scroll further down. Another video. This time, it's me lurching at Amber like a crazy lady, my face twisted in fury.

"Who filmed this?" I snivel.

I look at the username. I don't recognise it. The videos have been uploaded anonymously. It could have been anyone! It definitely wasn't The Witches; they're in the video with me, so it must have been someone who I thought was my *friend*.

I've never felt so humiliated in my life. But it doesn't stop there. My dad is the star of the final video that I can bear to watch. I relive the moment he skids into the living room with the slipper, scaring the partygoers away while food flies past and confetti flitters around him.

I can't believe this.

I'm about to slam Nyah's phone down on the bed in distress, but something catches my eye.

It's a name. A familiar name. My heart skips a beat when I realise whose name it is.

Daniel.

He's written a comment under the video of my dad.

Daniel07 · 2 minutes ago
hahahaha this is crazy!

My body goes hot, then it goes cold. The tears I thought I had cried out sneak back into my eyes and drip down my cheeks.

"Guys... Daniel has commented on this video," I whimper.

"Wasn't he supposed to come?" Nyah asks.

I roll my eyes. *Now's not the time for silly questions, Nyah.*

"Let me see!" Georgia squints at the phone.

She takes it from my limp hand and inspects the screen closely. She tuts and shakes her head. "Why would he *do* that?"

"You tell me!" I cry. "I'm so embarrassed."

First, he doesn't show up, and now he's *laughing* at me and my insane family. Could this birthday get ANY worse? Georgia and Nyah fall silent. There's nothing they can say that would make me feel any better right now. I'm a social media sensation, but for all the WRONG reasons. And to think I was glad that Daniel wasn't here to witness my disaster of a party. He'll be able to see it forever, now!

All the anger I had towards The Witches simmers back to the surface. I still can't believe they managed to swan into my party and single-handedly DESTROY it in less than an hour. They got what they wanted, and now I'll never be able to live this down. My thirteenth year is DOOMED from here on out!

"It's okay, Nonny. Like we said, no one will even care about this on Monday," Nyah says.

"That's not true! How can anyone forget anything like this?"

"Stop looking at the comments! You're just making yourself feel worse."

But I can't stop. I tap, tap, tap until a stream of comments fill the screen.

Scottyboi12 · 14 minutes ago

This is jokes!!! So sad I missed this lol

Dreamgirl · 16 minutes ago

this is soooooooooo embarrassing omg!!!

Lelah.smith · 19 minutes ago

I can't believe this actually happened

Chichi_ · 23 minutes ago

omg I was there when this happened! Soooo funny hahaha

Ughhhh – this is by far the WORST day of my life. The only thing that went right is the playlist me and my besties put together all those weeks ago, but we couldn't even enjoy *that* in the end.

Remind me to warn Isaac to never, ever host a party here. Ever.

"Come on, Nonny. Give me my phone. Let's go to sleep," Nyah says, softly.

She coaxes the phone from my hand and tucks it under the pillow.

"Good night, guys," Georgia whispers, reaching over my motionless body to turn the lamp off yet again.

"Good night," Nyah replies.

I say nothing.

Soon, they're both fast asleep. But I can't even close my eyes right now. I toss and turn, replaying the chaos over and over again, even though I know I shouldn't. It's like when you watch a scary movie and cover your eyes with your hands, but still peek through the gaps in your fingers.

After another painful half an hour, I eventually drift off.

I had imagined Sunday morning to be so different.

Me and my besties would wake up feeling on top of the world from last night, and I'd open the curtains to another lovely, sunny day. We'd stay in bed for hours, reliving my fabulous party. We'd flick through the hundreds of pictures and videos we captured, reminisce on how great our playlist was, and chat about how much we ate, laughed and danced. Then, we'd skip downstairs into the kitchen, where we'd load our bellies with leftover cake and uneaten party food.

But that doesn't happen.

As soon as I wake up on Sunday morning, yesterday's events hit me like a tonne of bricks. It feels like I've been punched in the gut. Not only is it raining, but Georgia and Nyah are still asleep. I don't blame them; they were up late last night helping me clean and trying to make me feel better.

I feel terrible.

There's no cake or leftover snacks in the kitchen for me, or a cheerful mum waiting to ask me if I enjoyed my party. Instead, I hear plates crashing and cupboard doors slamming. Whoever is in the kitchen is *angry*. I'm not leaving my room all day.

I hear the doorbell ring and I quickly peep out the window to see who it is. It's the DJ.

He must be back to collect the equipment he abandoned in a hurry yesterday. I feel sorry for him; I just know he'll be quivering in his boots while my mum towers over him, watching him pack up his equipment.

"Morning, Nonny," Nyah yawns, bringing me back to the room. She stretches. "You okay?"

I nod. I'm lying, of course. But I don't want her to feel any worse for me, so I have to pretend I'm much better.

"I'm fine." I force a weak smile.

"Good. Erm… I'm gonna get ready to go home if that's okay."

Nooooo, don't go!

My heart rate speeds up and a lump forms in my throat, but I don't make it obvious. I nod again. "Yeah, that's fine. Don't worry."

She smiles at me, gets out of bed and patters around the room to collect her things.

Don't wake Georgia up, I wish. I need someone to stay with me for a little bit longer.

I silently beg Georgia to keep snoring for at least another hour. But I guess that's too much to ask, because she soon rolls over and rubs her eyes.

"How long have you guys been awake?"

"Not long," Nyah and I say in unison.

"Are you leaving, Nyah?" Georgia asks.

Nyah looks guiltily at me, then back at Georgia. She nods. I hold my breath.

Don't say anything, Georgia. Don't say anything.

"I'd better get ready too, then," she says.

I feel my body crumple, but I take a deep breath. "No worries," I smile.

I watch them pack their clothes. I wish I could go with them, back to their warm, loving homes and kind parents who let them do anything they want. I bet if this had happened to either of them, their parents would scoop them up in a huge bear hug and tell them that everything would be okay.

But then again, this *wouldn't* happen to anyone but me.

"Okay, see you tomorrow then, Nonny," Nyah says, cheerily.

"Thank you for yesterday, guys. I love you both so much."

"You're welcome, Nonny. We love you, too," Georgia beams.

"You'll be okay, Nonny. Watch one of your shows or read a book to take your mind off it," Nyah suggests.

I nod.

"Do you really think everyone will forget about this?" I ask, knowing exactly what my besties will say but still wanting to hear them say it.

"One hundred percent. I bet Lucy Rimsdale will do something even *more* crazy this weekend. You know she always does," Nyah chuckles.

"Yeah, exactly. Everyone will be over this by tomorrow. And if they're not, you know we've always got your back. They'll have to get through *us* first."

I want to point out that *nobody* is threatened by us in the slightest, but I'm grateful for my friends trying to make me feel better.

"Thank you," I smile.

"We're gonna go now, Nonny. Please feel better."

"Yeah, and whatever you do, *don't* read those silly comments. They're all rubbish!"

"I won't, I promise."

My besties come over to give me a hug. I think we all know that I won't be seeing them out.

"Bye," I call, as the door shuts behind them.

When I hear the front door slam, I fall back

on my bed and exhale. I feel like a lost puppy without them here. But if anything is going to make me feel better right now, it's my shoebox of stones or Isaac.

I kneel on the carpet and stretch my arm underneath my bed to drag the box closer. I almost feel bad that, yesterday, I nearly abandoned my stones forever. I find my Magic Stone immediately and grasp it firmly. It fits perfectly in the palm of my hand, weighing it down only slightly. Here's to hoping it gives me some sort of superpower to wipe yesterday's events from everyone's memories – including mine!

I wait.

On any other day, I'd feel a weight lifted off my shoulders straightaway. But today is different.

Sigh.

Who am I kidding? I toss it into the box, put

the lid back on, and push the box back into the deep, dark void under my bed.

Isaac will do a better job of brightening my day. I tiptoe out of my room and go into his, on a mission to avoid any contact with my parents. His bright smile always cheers me up when I'm feeling down. When I enter, he's kneeling on the carpet, playing with his mini train set.

"Hey, Isaac," I whisper, sitting cross-legged beside him.

"Hi, Nonny!" he chirrups, handing me one of his beloved trains. I take it and move it sluggishly along the colourful tracks. "Choo, choo! Choo, choo!" he sings.

Noticing that I'm not doing the same, he tugs at my hand, his huge, brown eyes pleading me to join in.

"Choo, choo! Choo, choo!" I chuckle. Isaac giggles joyfully. I love playing with him. Sometimes, I'll pick him up and we'll pretend that he's a superhero, flying high above the city and saving everyone who's in trouble. I can't pick him up as easily as I used to, though. He eats EVERYTHING. Plus, he has the chubbiest cheeks that I *love* to squeeze, and podgy little hands that grab mine for comfort. Little does he know, he's my comfort too.

After a few minutes of playing and chatting, I get into his bed and close my eyes. Hopefully I can have a nice, peaceful nap and forget about how rubbish I feel for a couple of hours.

I float into the Land of Nod and sleep blissfully for what feels like days. When I finally wake up, it's nearly two o'clock in the afternoon.

As I pull the duvet tighter around me, I can sense someone lingering on the landing. I hear my bedroom door creak open, then shut. Ugh – one of my parents is looking for me. I slide further underneath the duvet, my heart hammering.

Please don't let it be my dad. Please don't let it be my—

"Nonny, wake up. Come and have some food." It's my mum.

I don't flinch or open my eyes even slightly. Pretending I'm asleep will usually make her go away. But not this time. As she sits on the bed, the mattress sinks. Just like my heart. She shakes my shoulder.

On Sunday afternoons, I'm usually watching TV, mucking around with Isaac or entertaining myself on the computer. She knows something's up.

"Come on, Nonny. I know you're upset about yesterday. Forget about it. You and your friends did a good job cleaning up. Now stop moping around and come and eat."

Forget about it? That's easy for her to say! Even though I'm glad her tone is no longer dripping in anger and she can actually stand to be around me, I'm still upset. She played a huge part in my ruining my party, too. It was her who cut off the music and ran upstairs to tattle to my dad – who, by the way, has *cemented* my future as a complete and utter laughing stock at school.

But… I *am* hungry.

And I guess this is her way of apologising, so I throw the covers back and follow her downstairs. Luckily, my dad's not at home. *Phew.*

I stare out of the window as I munch on a spoonful of rice. "Where's dad? I gulp.

"He's visiting your uncle."

I pause.

"Do you still hate me?"

My mum tuts. "Don't be silly. You're my child. I don't *hate* you."

"Yeah, but you're mad at me because of

yesterday."

"Just because I'm mad at you doesn't mean I hate you."

"It feels like it," I say quietly.

"The living room was a mess and your hooligan friends have no respect for nice things or their elders. I don't want any of them in this house again. But I don't hate you, Nonny. Eat your food."

"I won't invite them again," I murmur, pushing my food around with my spoon. I really mean it.

"The neighbours were NOT happy. You should have known better than to bring those awful people into our house."

I desperately want to correct her and let her know that, actually, it was *her* who let The Witches in, but I hold my tongue.

"Yes, mum."

Today's turning out to be a better day than

when it first started. My dad's not here and my mum no longer hates me, so that's good.

Now, I just have to get through tomorrow.

Monday morning rolls around faster than you can say "Disaster Birthday Party".

Great, another day of willing the ground to swallow me whole. I trudge downstairs, ready to convince my mum that I'm *way* too ill to go to school. Even though my acting skills are awesome, it NEVER works. But I have hope that, after this weekend's chaos, she'll have mercy on me today.

Before I reach the kitchen door, I pause in the hallway, preparing myself. I clear my throat to practise my BEST croaky voice and screw my face into a pained frown.

"I don't feel well, mum," I moan. *Hmmm, not moany enough.*

"I feel ill, mum," I whine. *Nope – I use this line WAY too much. She'll say no before I even open my mouth.*

"Mum, can I stay at home? I don't feel well." *Argh – too many words. Time is ticking, Nonny, just get on with it!*

I exhale slowly and enter the kitchen. My mum's cutting toast into small squares for Isaac.

"*Muuuum*... I feel sick," I cough.

I rest my hand on my forehead, faking a painful headache.

She inspects me closely with her eyes narrowed. But before she can answer, my dad barges into the kitchen in his suit, clutching a leather briefcase.

"You're going to school," he orders.

"But I'm *ill!*" I plead.

"So you want to destroy your future as well as our house? Go to school."

And just like that, he high-fives Isaac, mutters "bye", and exits the kitchen as quickly as he entered.

My mum raises her eyebrows. "You heard him. Go and get ready," she shrugs.

"This is so *unfair!*" I whinge.

"*Life* is unfair, Nonny. Now, stop moaning and go to school."

Before my party, I was extra careful to stop whining so I wouldn't aggravate my parents. But now that it's over, I can't help it! Would *you* want to go back to school after you threw the WORST party in the history of parties?

I get ready as slowly as I possibly can, trying

to prepare myself for all the pointing and whispers that I'm about to face. Before I leave, I envelop Isaac in a huge hug for good luck, take a deep, deep breath, and then make my way to school.

Beads of sweat trickle from my hairline as I reach the gates. It's not even that hot. I'm just so frightened to walk into the building where all eyes will be on me. I *loved* the attention at the beginning of my party; I felt like a princess, a queen, a STAR. But now? I just want to be invisible.

I'm late, so Georgia and Nyah aren't waiting for me at our usual spot. I drag my feet in the corridor, keeping my head down, my chin bumping against my chest. If I can't see anyone, they can't see me, right?

But as I turn the corner to get to my form room, I see The Witches.

Lurking.

My stomach heaves. *Oh no* – they must be waiting for me! I try to back away silently, but I've been spotted.

"Look, Becky! There's that crazy FREAK who tried to scratch my eyes out!" Amber thunders, charging towards me with Becky in tow.

I try to get away, but they swoop in on me like vultures ready to kill. Amber grabs my collar, pulling me towards her like a rag doll. I have no choice but to turn around. When I do, I'm face to face with the Head Witch.

Gulp.

My eyes immediately travel to the bright red wound on her cheek. I grimace. "S-sorry for scratching you, Amber," I mumble.

"Ha! Not so tough *now,* are you?" she sneers.

"I-I wasn't trying to be tough."

"I told my mum what you did and she's coming for you. So, you better watch out."

"I'm *sorry*, Amber," I wail.

If her mum is anything like her, she'll probably chop me up into little pieces and feed me to her witchy friends for dinner.

"You better be. And your party was RUBBISH, just like I thought it would be."

That stings, even though I know she's just trying to hurt my feelings.

"Just leave me alone," I mutter.

I try to push past her but Becky steps forward to block me.

Where are my friends when I need them?

"Where do you think you're going?"

"I need to get to my class," I plead.

Amber looks at Becky and gives her a quick nod. Becky does as she's told and moves out of my way. I scuttle away at top speed before they change their minds, not looking back once. I only breathe when I turn the corner.

"This isn't over, loser!" Amber calls after me.

I run straight past the classroom I'm supposed to be in, my shoes pounding on the floorboards, and head straight for the toilet. I lock myself in the cubicle right at the end and crouch on the lid, hugging my knees to my chest.

Ughhh – this place *reeks* of soggy P.E. socks dunked in the canned tuna my dad loves to eat.

"Ewwww," I mouth, feeling nauseous.

I don't know how long I'm going to last cooped up in this small, smelly space, but it's sure better than being out *there* with everyone laughing at me. News spreads faster than fire at school, especially when it's already all over the internet! I wouldn't be surprised if even the *teachers* have heard how much of a disaster my party was.

I don't want anyone to know I'm here, not even my best friends.

It's bad enough that The Witches are out to get me, but do you know who I'm *really* worried about seeing? Daniel! I'm dreading the moment we bump into each other. And that's exactly why I'm going to stick to this toilet seat like glue until breaktime. My next lesson is Maths – the only lesson we have together – and I just can't BEAR to see him.

I read all the bad words and insults on the

cubicle door over and over again to pass the time. By the time the bell rings, I can recite the rude, three-stanza poem about Mr Davies word for word. I also know that Sarah loves Fred, Kemi loves Josh and Clara HATES Zoe.

I reluctantly get to my feet… it's time to face the music. As I'm about to unlock the cubicle door, I hear two sets of footsteps getting closer. I step back and hold my breath.

"Did you see all the videos at the weekend?"

My breath catches in my throat.

They must be talking about me! I'm about two seconds away from diving head-first into the toilet and flushing myself into oblivion.

"Yeah! I can't believe that actually happened!"

I bite my lip so hard it might bleed. I wait for the raucous laughter.

But nothing.

"I know, poor Nonny. Her party was so

much fun, as well."

Wait. WHAT?

My mouth falls open in shock and my eyes almost pop out of my skull.

"It was *so* much fun. Whoever posted those videos is really mean."

Rachel and Grace finish what they're doing and pitapat away. I sit back down on the toilet lid, shocked, confused, but... *happy.* They didn't giggle at how embarrassing my party was. They didn't gossip about how crazy my parents are. In fact, they said they had *fun.*

I feel as light as a feather.

Maybe, just maybe, I can get through the day. Just as long as I can avoid Daniel and The Witches *like the plague.*

I creep out of the cubicle, my chest a little less tight than it was this morning, and join Georgia and Nyah in the canteen. They run to me when they see me.

"There you are! Are you okay, Nonny? We missed you this morning!" Georgia pants.

"I'm okay," I say.

This time, I'm not lying. I'm actually okay. The words I heard in the toilet were just what I needed. I still feel a little nervous, though. Georgia and Nyah shield me like bodyguards as we walk through the hall to get to our usual table. I clutch my juice carton so tight my knuckles might burst through my skin. I could be imagining it, but I can feel judgemental stares cutting into me from every direction.

"Don't worry, Nonny. No one's looking," Nyah whispers.

I know she's lying. I keep my eyes on the ground, but I'm sure that even the people who weren't invited to my party are snickering, pointing and looking right at me. We sit down and I gnaw absentmindedly on my chocolate chip cookie.

"We're glad you're okay, Nonny. I bet everyone's forgotten about those silly videos online. Anyway, I posted *loads* of photos of us three and *Daniel* has liked all of them," Nyah smirks, wiggling her eyebrows at me.

Even though that lifts my spirits, I feel the blood rush to my face at the sound of his name. Ugh, let's hope I don't see him anytime soon. A hand taps me lightly on the shoulder. I freeze.

Daniel?

A freckled face and hazel eyes come into view and I exhale unsteadily. It's Frankie; she was at my party. I can barely look at her.

"Hey Nonny, are you okay?"

I nod, slowly, waiting for the sniggers to follow.

"I just wanted to say how much fun I had at your party. A-and I'm really sorry that I messed it up by throwing all that food. It must have been really hard to clean up."

"Err... thanks... I..." I'm lost for words.

"It *was* really hard, actually. We were up all night, scrubbing like slaves!" Georgia jumps in, exaggerating.

They continue talking while I stare into space. Maybe my friends were right. Maybe everyone *will* forget about what happened on Saturday.

Frankie walks away and Georgia's and Nyah's grinning faces come into focus.

"*See*, Nonny?" Nyah chortles.

"Did you hear what Frankie just said, Nonny?"

I shake my head.

"She said that all the girls from French said your party was the best party they've been to for ages! And that they're all really sorry. *See?* No one cares!" Georgia declares.

I snap out of my trance. *"Really?"*

My besties nod crazily, like those funny, big-headed toys on car dashboards. Above their heads, I notice The Witches loitering nearby. Amber's face is crimson with rage and Becky's mouth is hanging open in disbelief. They overheard the entire conversation, and they are *not* happy. HA!

I can finally manage a sunny smile.

Home time comes, and I have a slight spring in my step again. My day wasn't as bad as I had expected. Firstly, I hadn't seen Daniel all day, which I NEVER thought I'd be happy about. Secondly, I *had* crossed paths with The Witches in the corridor again after lunch, who were obviously SO angry that their plans to turn me into the biggest joke of Year Eight had backfired. When they saw me this time, all they did was glare in my direction and mime that they were "coming for me".

I'm super worried, of course, but that's a drama for another day. Besides, The Witches can't bring me down any further than I already have been the last few days. They can say and do whatever they want – they always have and they always will. And I'm sure Amber's mum is scary, but *my* mum is scarier. Which *everyone* now knows.

I hurry towards the big glass doors, ready to push through them into freedom.

But then someone calls my name.

I stop dead in my tracks. I know that voice.

It's Daniel!

Do I pretend I haven't heard him and keep walking? Or do I turn around and face him? Ahhh, I can't bear to! I look dreadful and tired, and I can feel my face getting warm with embarrassment. *I can't let him see me like this. I can't—*

"Erm, hi, Nonny," Daniel sputters sheepishly, interrupting my frantic thoughts.

Too late.

But wait... he knows my name now! Oh my gosh... OH MY GOSH!

My knees wobble. They just might give way any second and I'll end up collapsing right in front of my ultimate crush!

"Hi, Daniel," I croak.

I clear my throat and swallow hard. I hope he can't see how jittery I am right now.

He takes a deep breath and looks down at his amazingly polished shoes. Is he... *nervous?*

"Sorry I didn't come to your party. I was really sick that day."

I have to stop myself from wrapping my arms around him and crushing his bones with the strongest hug I've ever given.

He didn't miss my party on purpose – he was *sick!* And he actually went out of his way to *apologise* to me. I beam as though I haven't been grieving over his absence since Saturday night.

"That's okay!"

"I keep hearing how good your party was. I

wish I had been there," he sighs.

WOOHOO!

I picture myself performing backflips and acrobatic stunts all over the school foyer. (Not exactly realistic, as I can only just about do a somersault in real life, but a girl can daydream.)

"Thanks," I reply, coolly. "It *was* fun." I pause. *Dare I say it?* "I… I wish you had been there, too."

I cringe inwardly as the words hang silently in the air.

He chuckles.

"I saw your dad online, as well. I thought that was so funny."

My heart stops.

No, no, NO! This is NOT how our first proper conversation is supposed to go!

Daniel must notice the horrified look on my face because he suddenly looks embarrassed.

"S-sorry, I-I don't mean to laugh. It's just that

the videos cheered me up while I was ill, that's all."

I relax a little and nod cautiously. That's okay... I guess.

"Well... I'm glad you're feeling better," I smile.

"Thanks, Nonny. See you tomorrow... in *Maths*." His head lolls back and he sticks his tongue out to the side, pretending to die of boredom. I laugh.

"Bye, Daniel."

I wave enthusiastically. And with that, he's gone. I sigh and lean against the wall as floods of people gush through the doors to head home. My heart skitters in my chest. EEEEK – that was the longest conversation we've *ever* had. *And* he had heard that my party was great! Double EEEEK!

Maybe thirteen *isn't* so doomed, after all.

Don't get me wrong, we all know that it

didn't get off to the *best* start. Now, whenever I look back on the day I turned thirteen, I'll cringe in despair. Flashbacks of my dream cake being PUSHED to the floor will creep up on me when I least expect it, haunting me for *years* to come. Images of the food-stained walls are now burned into my brain, and I just *know* they'll continue to send hot shudders down my spine *forever*. And who could forget the SUPER HUMILIATING clip of my dad plastered across the internet with confetti in his beard, his vein popping in his temple, and his face screwed up in anger?

But I'll also ALWAYS remember my two best friends telling me that everything will be fine, helping me clear up for hours and rubbing my back while I sob uncontrollably. If I didn't have them then, and didn't have them now, I don't think I'd be able to show my face at school *ever again*. Now I know that I can get through

ANYTHING with my best friends by my side, even fighting with The Witches!

And though I know that *some* people are still sniggering behind their hands and babbling about how NUTS me and my family are, most people were really kind and said that they LOVED my party, which makes everything ten times better!

I follow the crowds of people plodding home and shade my eyes with my hand as the sun dazzles and shines. I don't know why, but right now, I just know that everything will be fine.

So… what should I do for my fourteenth birthday?